*Harlequin
Presents..*

KARIN MUTCH

cindy, tread lightly

HARLEQUIN BOOKS
toronto-winnipeg

© Karin Mutch 1969

Original hard cover edition published in 1969
by Mills & Boon Limited

SBN 373-70566-2
Harlequin Presents edition published October 1974

Printed in Canada.

CHAPTER ONE

'OH, HEAVENS!' Cindy Taylor stopped running and glanced up and down the street. Which street, she hadn't the faintest idea. She was lost.

Friday night traffic zoomed by her as she stood on the corner of the street waiting for the lights to turn, and people jogged and hustled against her until she was forced to the very edge of the gutter.

She gave a helpless little groan and bit hard on her lower lip. Her first week in the Queen City and she was lost. Up until a half-an-hour ago she hadn't been in the least afraid, but the chilly early-winter rains began to fall unexpectedly and she was now soaking wet and shivering cold. Her new winter frock clung to her like a second skin and her long brown hair was plastered against her scalp and neck.

She stood on the side of the pavement where the rain bounced into the deep, light-reflected puddles. Clutching against her the bunch of long-stemmed chrysanthemums which she had bought on the spur of the moment, she strove to catch sight of an unoccupied taxi, but as it was a Friday night, a late shopping night, she realized that she didn't have much hope of finding one.

Suddenly she felt, rather than heard, a car swerve around the corner alongside of her. The wind coming from the swift speed of the vehicle whipped her wet frock against her thighs and before she could step back from the gutter's edge, the front wheels of the car had splashed through a dark muddy puddle causing a thick gush of grey water to spray up over the front of her frock.

Horrified, she glanced down at the greyish stain. This was too much. The big city, bright lights and thronging crowds which had appealed to her in the beginning, were slowly losing their charm and glamour. She was almost wishing she had never left her tiny country home-town.

But it would never do if she broke down right here in this busy thoroughfare, so with a lift of her chin she glared balefully through the dim interior at the driver of the car, who had stopped and opened the door.

'Sorry about that, honey. Are you waiting for someone?'

Cindy shook her head miserably and cast another glance down at her frock.

'Then you'd better hop in.'

Cindy started and stiffened. 'No, thanks. I'm waiting for a taxi.'

'You'll be waiting here all night. You're soaking wet. Come on, get in. I can't stay parked here forever.'

At any other time Cindy wouldn't have spoken to a strange man, much less get into a car with one. However, right then she was too cold and miserable to care and, besides, cars coming up behind them were honking their horns impatiently. Clinging tightly to her bag and rain-beaten flowers, she slid into the car next to the stranger.

'Here, wrap this around you.' He reached over to the back seat and thrust a woollen rug on to her lap. 'What kind of fool would stand out in that downpour dressed like that?'

With her teeth chattering with cold she did as she was told and managed to say clearly enough: 'It wasn't raining earlier on. In fact there wasn't a cloud in the sky.'

He turned the car into a side street and headed in a direction away from the main shopping areas. 'Surely you have brains enough to realize that one can't go by that at this time of year? No, apparently you haven't. What's your name?'

'Cindy Taylor.' She looked at him in the fleeting orange glare of the street light but saw only a shadowy outline of his profile. 'What's yours?'

'Stuart Newman.'

'Where — where are you taking me? I live out at Browns Bay.'

'I'm taking you to my place.'

At once a wave of panic swept over her. 'If you don't mind, I'd rather you took me straight home.'

'If you stay in those clothes much longer you'll more than likely get pneumonia.'

'Please, there's no need for you to bother.'

'It's no bother.' He turned and she saw his teeth flash white in the darkness and she knew that he was smiling at her.

Involuntarily she shivered and moved back against the hard frame of the door. What was she going to do? What could she do in a situation such as this?

'Don't worry, Cindy Taylor, I have no evil intentions. I don't plan to abduct you. It's just that I'm in the mood for a little company and that of a stranger should make an interesting change. In fact, I'm sure it will.'

However, this assurance did very little to ease her fear. Why on earth did she consent to get into his car? 'Do you usually take what you want without consulting the other person involved?' Cindy asked coldly, her hands tense in her lap, clenching the flower stems. 'Especially when the other person is a stranger?'

He laughed — a soft deep sound, deliberately provoking, giving the interior of the car a close intimate atmosphere which Cindy didn't care for. 'Especially when the stranger involved is a female — regardless of the fact that she looks more like a drenched, scared rabbit.'

He drove the rest of the way to his residence without speaking. He pulled up outside his home, a modern house set well back from the road and a large garden which harboured many huge trees. The whole section was surrounded by a high wooden fence.

He switched off the engine and the steady purr receded followed by silence. Lighting up a cigarette he sat smoking it, letting his eyes rove over her in the semi-darkness.

Cindy remained staring in front of her, her nerves tautened to snapping point as the silence grew. How was she going to get out of this entanglement? She hadn't had much experience of men and especially not men like Stuart Newman, a city man, a man who she was sure was worldly and experienced and knew all the angles when it came to women.

Slowly, with catlike movements, he was out of the car and around her side helping her out.

With a mutter of impatience he pulled the flowers from her hands and flung them carelessly into the garden. 'For a start you can get rid of these damn things.'

'Oh — my flowers!' The cry broke from her lips and automatically she made to go and retrieve them but was thwarted by Stuart's hard hand on her shoulder.

'They've had it — broken,' he said, and it seemed to her that he found pleasure in telling her so.

'You — you beast!'

'Oh, what the hell! They're only flowers. Come on, the door is this way.'

She sensed a kind of ruthlessness about him. A ruthlessness of touch, manner and determination in that nothing should or would stand in his way. A man who took what he wanted regardless and not counting the cost. 'You're a cruel man, aren't you?'

He was rather taken aback at the quiet directness of her question, then recovering from his momentary surprise he smiled. Cindy could tell by the tone of his voice. 'I can be both cruel and kind and, to defenceless little babies like you, I'm as kind as I know how.'

'Somehow I find that hard to believe.'

'You're a smart little cookie, aren't you?'

'As smart as I know how,' she replied solemnly.

Then he laughed with genuine amusement. 'Honey, you're going to prove to be a companion I think I'm going to like having around.'

'I'm sorry to have to disappoint you, but I don't plan to be around long enough for you to find out.'

'You're forgetting that I'm a man who gets what he wants and you'll find that I'm a very impatient man.' He unlocked the door and motioned her to go in before him.

As she entered the dark interior of the hall she felt his arm move, and for a terrifying second she thought he was going to grab her. Blindly she darted away from him and immediately felt the hard impact of a low table, which was resting against the wall, strike against her thigh. Simultaneously pale light flooded through the hall and she found herself blinking at him, her eyes wide with pain and surprise. He was grinning at her with sardonic amusement. 'I'm not as primitive as all that. As you can see, I was merely going to put on the light so that you wouldn't trip over that table and break your neck.'

'Oh.' She was beginning to feel foolish. Was she seeing things into this situation that weren't there at all, but only in her imagination?

'You sound rather disappointed. Don't I come up to your expectations of being an abductor?' He made a movement towards her and immediately she flattened herself against the wall. 'Maybe I can correct that impression.' His voice was low and his face much too close to hers.

'No!' She tried to move sideways, away from the table, but found that she was imprisoned by his arms placed each side of her, his hands on the wall.

'But that's what you wanted — wasn't it?'

'You know quite well it wasn't, you great . . .' Even to her own ears her voice sounded breathless and her protest feeble. What on earth was happening to her? Those eyes were smiling so deeply and brilliantly they were almost hypnotizing her. 'I'm not that kind — kind of girl.' Why she added that remark, she didn't know. She only knew that she had to say something — and quickly.

He shook his head slowly. 'Every girl is that kind of girl given the chance. Every girl wants to be good but at the same time longs to be bad.'

She stared at him for a minute and then stuttered: 'You're mad!' This was riduculous! Now she knew how Alice in Wonderland must have felt in her dream, going from one crazy episode to another. The only difference was that this was no dream.

'Please let me go.' Desperately she began to plead with him. His closeness was beginning to fuddle her brain somehow so that she couldn't think clearly.

Then somewhere from behind him a voice spoke. 'Mr. Newman . . . Oh, I'm sorry, I just heard you come in. I didn't realize you weren't alone.'

Taking his time, Stuart lowered his arms and, with a faint sob of thankfulness, Cindy closed her eyes and breathed a sigh of relief. But deep within her something told her that she had actually uttered a sigh which came closer to being one of disappointment than of relief. Her eyes flew open and she stared, horrified, into those glittering ones still close to hers.

'You see what I mean?' he whispered and, straightening up, he moved away from her and turned to face the woman who had interrupted them. 'Don't go, Elizabeth. This is Cindy Taylor and as you can see she's wet to the skin. Would you light the fire in the lounge and I'll see that she changes out of those wet clothes so that you'll be able to dry them. Cindy, this is my housekeeper, Elizabeth Reefton.'

'How do you do?' Elizabeth nodded briefly. Her face was as expressionless as was her voice.

Cindy could do nothing — say nothing. She was burning with embarrassment at sensing this older woman's disapproval and perhaps distaste as she turned back to Stuart. 'Would you like me to prepare supper?'

'Yes, if you would. The child looks as though she could do with a bite to eat. You can change in the bathroom, Cindy, and I'll find you something to put on.'

Instinctively, Cindy hung back. She looked at Elizabeth appealingly, but already Elizabeth was making her way to what must have been the lounge.

Stuart laughed, 'You won't find help in that direction, my fair captive. Elizabeth is as loyal as they come and never says a word out of place.'

She was helpless and she knew it, but gallantly Cindy drew herself up and glared at him. 'How dare you let her believe that I — I was a — tramp!'

'Do you think that she believed that? I thought that she did remarkably well in hiding her thoughts behind an expressionless mask.'

'She's probably used to having you bring a girl-friend home for the night. She didn't bat an eyelid and that's why I knew she believed it and what's more so did you.'

Stuart shrugged. 'Well, we can't go and enlighten her about you just yet. She just might become disillusioned. Come on and I'll show you where the bathroom is.' He took hold of her wrist.

Shaking off his hand, she sent him a look of pure dislike and went on a little ahead of him up the thickly carpeted hall.

In spite of her calamity, she couldn't help being impressed with the part of the house she had seen so far. It spelt bachelor with a capital B. The design was modern and spacious and furnished sparsely with red-brown wooden furniture to match narrow skirtings, doors and window frames. The wallpapers were pale and plain with which the carpets, curtains and other furnishings teamed superbly in colours of dark green, gold and brown.

He must be wealthy, she decided, to be able to possess such a home and marvellously landscaped grounds. Although there were thousands in Auckland equally luxurious, they usually housed middle-aged couples with families or retired couples.

'This is the bathroom.' Stuart stopped and opened a door leading into a neat bathroom, cold in black, white and gold but smelling pleasantly of soaps, toothpaste and clean towels like most bathrooms mingled with the tangy fragrance of male aftershave and hair dressing.

Cindy went in, her shoes tapping hollowly on the tiles. She looked around and then back at Stuart who was leaning against the door frame. He was big, six feet or more, with wide shoulders, slimmer hips and long strong legs which made Cindy think that he had been a keen rugby player at one stage. He was wearing dark slacks and a white bulky pullover which seemed to emphasize his size.

Suddenly Cindy was visited by a sensation of adventure, exciting and at the same time frightening. She was afraid of the unknown but felt drawn towards it and at the age when she felt a strong desire to tempt fate and find and experience the other side of life, of which, so far, she had hardly seen a glimpse.

Stuart straightened from his lounging position and disappeared and a moment later came back into the bathroom and thrust a large clean towel at her. 'Get in and have a shower and dry yourself with this. I'll go and get something for you to put on. Leave your wet things outside the door.'

Cindy stood alone in the bathroom, undecided what she should do. 'What if he should come back in again?' she thought. She wouldn't put it past him. After a few more minutes had gone by, she presumed that she would be left in peace and commenced undressing. As he requested she dropped the discarded clothes outside the door.

'Now, Elizabeth, don't give me that frown of disapproval and "what is to become of you" look. I'm quite old enough to look after myself,' Stuart mocked laughingly as he entered the kitchen and deposited Cindy's clothes into Elizabeth's waiting arms.

'So you say — however, I sometimes wonder,' Elizabeth rejoined dryly.

'Well?'

'Well what?'

'You usually give me your opinions of my "latest" as you call them, before I have time to ask.' Stuart followed her into the lounge and watched as she folded the clothes over a rack and propped it in front of the blazing fire. He lit a cigarette and waited interestedly for her answer.

'Yes, I do, but usually they are much older and experienced and know themselves what they're doing — much more capable of protecting themselves against men like you, if they want to, than that youngster.'

Stuart nodded. 'I agree, as always, because you're right as always. But I'm afraid older and more sophisticated women are beginning to bore me. It suddenly hit me just how bored I've become when I saw Cindy Taylor tonight, staring at me balefully from those huge blue eyes of hers after I had just added a spray of muddy water on to her already soaking frock. I thought to myself: "Now there's a picture of inexperience — innocence. This should prove to be both a refreshing and interesting change." '

'Well, if she was ready to come home with a stranger, a man like you, so willingly, then to my mind she's not too innocent.'

Stuart laughed. 'Believe me, she wasn't willing — just resigned. Anyway I don't think she has ever come across men like me. In her world men are still just people like her father, brother and uncle, etcetera.'

'Then, if that's the case, leave the girl alone. Don't turn her into another Delia just to satisfy your own whims.'

Stuart's face darkened at the mention of Delia. 'No girl can be turned into anything unless she's willing and wants it that way,' he snapped harshly.

But to Elizabeth Reefton his anger was like water on a duck's back.

'If it's any comfort to you and if it'll reassure you that I haven't gone completely to the bad, I promise you I have no intention of having an affair with the girl against her will. I'll probably be bored to death by her anyway, as soon as the novelty has worn off.'

'Look, you're a big hunk of man, attractive and charming. What girl wouldn't be swept off her feet and be swept away by that charm — which would later mean nothing to you but could wreck her whole life. I saw her tonight after a dosing of that charm. The poor thing looked frightened and bewildered but at the same time excited, aware of experiencing something new and different, puzzling but at the same time wonderful. For a girl it's wonderful to be swept off her feet by any man but tragic if it's the wrong man. Leave her unscarred for the right man and stick to someone of Delia's sort where vulnerable emotions and feelings so vital and important to the young aren't involved . . .'

'Oh, good grief, Elizabeth! Stop preaching to me like some plurry Churchman trying to give me a conscience, and don't keep dragging Delia into all our conversations. Just leave her out of it. All I want to do is to forget her and if someone like Cindy Taylor is the road to forgetting, then I'll use it, regardless of whether she's so damn young and innocent.'

With a sigh Elizabeth watched him slam out of the lounge, silently cursing herself and Delia Lawrence. Elizabeth had been employed by Stuart for five years and, during that time, although they didn't see eye to eye on many subjects and argued on and off, they got along famously, their relationship resting on more of a friendly basis than an employer-employee basis.

She had known him many years before she came to work for him and so knew that he had been hurt and disillusioned by various incidents and people in his life, and she was personally familiar with his affairs with different women and his relationship with Delia Lawrence. She knew she didn't have the right to proffer her advice but often did, for she felt sure that he was, being too proud to ask her straight out, mentally, rather than verbally asking for it. She sensed his needs and knew that despite his anger he was glad of her straight-from-the-shoulder attitude towards him.

After dressing in a knee-length bathrobe made of thick white towelling and tied around the middle by a length of white cord, Cindy slipped her feet into a pair of fluffy slippers and followed Stuart's instructions and found her way to the lounge.

Stuart looked around from his position facing the fire and watched her standing nervously on the thick, creamy coloured carpet, twisting the cord of the bathrobe between her fingers. She was a tall slender girl with a slight bust and gently curving hips. Her legs were long and by the line of her thighs and what

15

could be seen from beneath the hemline of the gown he could see they were nicely shaped.

Her hair was drier and a little tangled for the want of a brush and comb and from her face he gained the impression that she was all eyes staring at him unwaveringly and a little afraid.

'Come in — closer to the fire. I'm not going to eat you.' He spoke impatiently and immediately the change of mood in him was made evident to Cindy — and it was a mood she liked much less than his previous one. His eyes were dark and moody and his mouth was set in hard lines. She shivered, again thinking he could be capable of ruthlessness and cruelty.

She was afraid but strove not to show it and crept closer to the fire and bent to hold her hands to the flames. As she did so, her face came level with a photograph of a very beautiful woman whose head was resting on the tip of her finger and her mouth was curved into a smile of what, to Cindy, looked like triumph.

She heard Stuart's sharp indrawn breath beside her and looking up she saw that he too was staring at the photograph.

'She — she's very beautiful,' Cindy felt she must say.

'She's a tramp!'

Cindy blinked and straightened up. 'Oh, no, she's too beautiful, like a mischievous angel.'

Stuart made a harsh sound in his throat which was supposed to be a laugh. 'She's no angel, nothing better than a tramp.'

Then before Cindy's startled eyes, Stuart picked up the photograph and threw it down on the hearth, smashing the frame into dozens of fragments. Slowly, he crouched down, shook the photo free of broken glass and dropped it into the fire and watched as the flames licked up around it curling it into ash, then, after a second or two, he got up and strode from the room.

Cindy hadn't moved from her position when he later re-entered the lounge carrying a tray of steaming coffee and toasted sandwiches. He placed the tray on a paua-shell inlaid table near the fire and shifted the sofa around to face it. He told her to sit down and handed her a mug of coffee.

'How old are you?' he asked after she was seated and sipping her coffee. There was nothing in his expression to tell her that he was brooding over what had happened a little while before.

'Twenty.'

'Stranger to Auckland?'

'Yes. How did you know?'

He raised an eyebrow at her as if to say: 'Are you kidding?' 'You have country written all over you, not because of your apparent inexperience, for I'm well aware that in some country towns people are more experienced in the ways of the world than they are in cities. Perhaps it's your complexion, the way you walk,' he shrugged, grinning at her lazily.

She laughed. 'The way I walk?' she repeated, feeling a little more at ease with him.

'Yes. A freer, more swinging stride, than the girls have here in the city. What part of the country are you from?'

'Manawatu, from a town called Apiti.'

He shook his head. 'I know the district very well, the Manawatu is very beautiful. Apiti must be one of those one-street towns out in the backblocks.

Cindy nodded, staring down at her face reflected in the dark ring of coffee. She swung her head around to look at him only to look away quickly, becoming increasingly flustered as the silence intensified. Her gaze rested on the broken glass on the hearth and impulsively she moved from the sofa and crouched to gather up the scattered pieces.

'Leave that!'

She jumped at his sudden sharp command and dropped the pieces she had in her hand back on to the neutral coloured brick hearth. Sitting back on the edge of the sofa she looked at him puzzled.

'If you start messing around there, you'll probably cut yourself. Elizabeth will see to it in the morning.'

'Where is she — Mrs. Reefton, I mean?' she asked, not really believing the reason he gave for his sharp exclamation.

'Retired to her own quarters for the night and at this moment I'd say she is probably watching some spine-chilling murder movie on television.'

'Well, sounds like a good way to wind up an evening and go to bed thinking about it,' Cindy laughed.

For a length of time there was silence and then she felt his whispered words fan against her cheek: 'You think so?' Almost against her will she turned and simultaneously he bent his head sideways and before she realized his intention she felt the hard unfamiliar form of his head and the roughness of his cheek buried between her neck and shoulder. His mouth moved along the side of her neck and then to the hollow of her shoulder, pushing away the collar of her bathrobe.

Taken completely by surprise, Cindy could do nothing for a few unforgettable seconds but remain passive, sitting rigid and numb. Then, before she could think of what she should do, Stuart abruptly lifted his head and moved away from her.

'I'm sorry.' He grinned at her wide-eyed unblinking expression, not looking at all sorry. 'I forgot my resolutions and promises for a moment.'

'I didn't think a person like you put much importance on such things as promises,' Cindy said icily, not really knowing what she was talking about. She clenched her hands together in her lap. She had never been kissed like that before — if it could be called a kiss — and it had unnerved her.

The only boy who had ever kissed her was her childhood friend Tony. Dear, faithful Tony who had asked her not to leave Apiti but to stay and marry him. Disappointed though he had been when she refused, he had wished her well and told her that he would always be waiting for her, whenever she decided to return.

Tony, whom she had known all her life, had never ventured to kiss her other than on her lips. Hesitant, shy, but tender, and here, Stuart Newman, whom she had known only a few short hours had taken the liberty to kiss her where she would never allow any man to kiss her unless they were engaged.

But this was Auckland, fast, lively and sophisticated, and this man was also fast and sophisticated. Did he expect her to be the same now that she had come to live in the city? Was it the expected thing?

For all her innocence and inexperience she knew what men like Stuart expected from women. Did he expect it from her? And what of this woman, whose photo was now nothing but smoke and ash? Where did she fit in? Cindy shook herself mentally. It was becoming all too dangerous and far more involved than she liked — more and more like an Alice in Wonderland dream.

She stood up and gathered her rather crumpled clothes from the rack beside her. 'I'd like to go home now. My clothes are dry. If you'll call me a taxi I'll be ready in about five minutes.'

Stuart looked up at her and noted the way she held her head and shoulders firmly back, at the line of her mouth and the glint in her eyes, uncertain and yet challenging him to dare and try and keep her there against her will. He knew that she had never been kissed like that before and even suspected that she had never really been kissed properly.

He wasn't at all repentant for his action, but he liked her quiet dignity and found it intriguing.

At first he had been prepared to take all he could get just out of spite to Delia and all women whom he vowed he would use only for his own convenience and pleasure, no other feelings involved.

But this was the first time a girl had reacted as Cindy had done and now as he watched her walk from the room he was visited by a strong urge to prove to himself that this girl was no different, no better than the rest, and to do that he had to turn her into another Delia. If she did succumb to him then he would know he was right. Gone were the rushes of intrigue and liking he had had for her. He only knew that he had to prove himself right, prove that he was right in distrusting the members of her sex.

'Have you rung a taxi?' Cindy asked, facing him in the hall now dressed in her crumpled stained frock.

'Of course not. I'll run you to your flat, or wherever it is you live, myself. Going to Browns Bay by taxi at this time of night will cost you a fortune.'

'Thanks.' She accepted and went out ahead of him to the Ford Falcon which was covered with sparkling rain drops. She slipped across on to the cold leather seat, suppressing a shiver, and waited for Stuart to start up the car.

For some time neither of them spoke as the car sped through the near deserted streets out towards Auckland's Harbour Bridge and Browns Bay. Everything was so bright and shiny it fascinated Cindy. Orange and pale blue street lights shone brilliantly along each side of the wide streets. Orange for the wider streets and pale blue for the narrower ones and all reflecting on the wet black surface of the road.

It was a long drive out to Browns Bay and Stuart

20

remarked: 'Aren't you a little far out? How do you get to work in the mornings or do you work out here?'

'I haven't found a job yet. I've only been here a week and accommodation is rather scarce so I had to take what was offering. I'll be moving in to board with my cousin and her husband at Mission Bay once they have the spare room ready.'

'Mission Bay is still rather far out, isn't it?'

'Yes, I guess so, but there will be buses running regularly.'

'And what kind of job are you looking for? What are your qualifications?'

'I'm a fully qualified shorthand-typist — nothing very exciting I'm afraid,' her tone unconsciously wistful.

'Are you looking for excitement, Cindy?'

She stiffened, fully alert once more. 'Not your brand of excitement, Mr. Newman.'

'What brand then?'

'I doubt whether you would understand or be interested.'

'Why not try me?'

Cindy opened her mouth to try and explain but gave a sigh instead. 'It's of no consequence. After tonight we'll never meet again, so what does it matter?'

'What makes you think we'll never meet again?'

'Isn't that obvious? We have nothing in common. There is no reason for our paths to cross again. Anyway, I think you're a man who is easily bored and not being up with the people you're used to mixing with, I'd bore you more quickly than anyone.'

'Uh-huh,' he shook his head, 'A change — you're a mixture of naiveté and wisdom, a refreshing change from what I'm used to. You've a lot to learn about men and this world you've opened to yourself. You need to be taught and I would prove to be a good teacher.'

'I have no doubts about that, but what I want to learn and what you want to teach me are two entirely different things.'

'What you want to be taught or what you're afraid to be taught?'

Cindy darted a look at him, beginning to feel angry. 'I'm not interested in affairs, Mr. Newman, if that's what you mean.'

'Aren't you? By the way your pulse was beating crazily at your throat when I kissed you I would have thought that, for a moment, just a moment, you were. You weren't immune anyway, were you?' He turned the car swiftly at her sharp instruction to turn left and stopped at the third house, a house which had been divided into two flats.

'What are you trying to do, Mr. Newman, boost that trampled masculine pride of yours? For I presume it has been trampled by that woman in the photograph. Do you want to use me to assure yourself that your charm hasn't lost its effect over the female?'

'I don't need to be assured of that!' With a sudden movement he took her upper arms and drew her across the space of upholstery to him. She stiffened instantly and struggled to resist him, but his hold was like bands of steel.

'Let me go!' Again despite her protests she felt herself turning weak as those compelling eyes smiled down into hers. Her heart thumped against her side as his thick lashes lowered and he gazed at her mouth. He bent his head and his mouth was just a whisper from her own when she felt his hand encircle her neck and his thumb rest against the hollow of her throat. His eyelids flickered up and he smiled triumphantly. 'See what I mean?' he murmured for the second time that night.

He let her go and was about to get out of the car when he heard the door on her side open and slam shut and saw her running figure disappear into the dark night.

CHAPTER TWO

TO VISIT Auckland had always been Cindy's chief ambition. Perhaps because fate had always, in some way or another, stopped her from going, she was all the more determined to fulfil her ambition.

So, following up her ever present sense of adventure, she made her break from home — Hawai Farm, situated some miles up into the Ranges away from the tiny town of Apiti which lay almost at the foot of the mountainous Ruahine Range.

To her, at home, life had always meant waking up before the sun, catching the school bus to the country school which had a total attendance of sixteen pupils. Later it meant boarding school in the country's capital, Wellington, before returning to her family and friends — and Tony.

Cindy knew only too well that her parents and Tony's parents wanted them to marry, but she hedged whenever the subject was brought up. She wasn't sure whether that was what she wanted but she did know that she wasn't ready to settle down. However, she was still content to attend the local functions with him; to the occasional barn or country club dances and visits to the local hall on Saturday where the movies were shown.

On Saturday mornings she would sit on the sideline and watch him play rugby in teams made up of all the young farmers in the district. They were tough men, big and vigorous who played hard and vigorous rugby known only to the backblocks. A case of either put your head down or get it knocked off.

Regardless of the fact that they owned powerful cars which were needed to deal with the mountainous rugged roads, some of the players jogged into town to play in the rain, cold or sleet, in mud ankle deep until one couldn't tell a Maori from a pakeha or one team from the other. After the game, they would pause only for a shower and a drink of beer before they began their jog back to their farms to resume their normal duties.

She would miss all this, the people and their nature and customs, their abusive language and their down to earth, take it or leave it, attitude towards life and people, anyone and everyone.

But that was one kind of life she already knew. Auckland offered her another totally different life — a difference which held her fascinated and compelled to stay.

Although Friday night's incident was still fresh in her mind, Cindy never really expected to meet up with Stuart Newman again. Auckland was a big city and out of its vast population it was hardly likely that she would, unless of course he made a point of contacting her and realizing that this possibility was not very probable she was glad but at the same time a vague hope that he would kept niggling at her until each time it arose she would thrust it impatiently out of her mind.

A week came and went and during that time she didn't have much opportunity to allow her thoughts to stray. After moving in with her cousin Jo and her husband, Keith, at their home situated on the hills lining Mission Bay, she began to search through the Situations Vacant columns of every newspaper with hope of finding a position that might appeal to her.

Finally, on the first Wednesday after she had moved in, an advertisement in the morning paper caught her eye:

Secretary to Hotelier required. Shorthand-typing essential and previous office experience preferred. Applicants must be prepared to travel. Interesting and varied work. Excellent salary. Telephone for an appointment: SOUTHERN CROSS HOTEL.

'That sounds just the thing,' Cindy thought. She had had no previous experience in an office but she was better than average at shorthand-typing. 'Well, there's no harm in trying,' she decided, and then hesitated for a moment. Should she wait and discuss it with Jo and Keith first? But then by the time they both arrived home from work the position would more than likely be filled and the opportunity would have passed her by.

So ringing through to the Hotel she made an appointment for an interview which was to be at three p.m. that afternoon.

She took a great deal of care over her appearance, for the more she thought about the position the more it appealed to her and the more determined she was to make the best of this opportunity.

At two-fifteen she was ready, dressed in a dark brown suit and an aqua blue blouse. Viewing herself critically in the mirror she was satisfied that she would create a good impression if nothing else.

'Ooops — goodness, is that the taxi already? Where the devil's my bag?' she muttered to herself, flustered, 'interview' nerves just beginning.

With her stomach feeling like one great twisted knot, Cindy stepped into the foyer of the new Auckland hotel, not a terrifically big hotel but an exclusive one. A splendid building oozing luxury — expensive luxury. Thick dark blue carpets sprawled before her throughout the wide reception with enormous flower arrangements in tall gold containers standing to fill various vacant corners.

Her heels sank into the carpet as she crossed to the widely curved reception desk. She waited while one of the receptionists rang through to inform the Hotelier that she had arrived and then followed the uniformed figure upstairs through a private and equally luxurious section of the hotel.

The office she was led into was spacious with only the necessary items of furniture, filing cabinets, chairs and one wide glass-topped desk placed on the same blue carpet. A man was standing looking out of the great span of window which looked out over some of the city and always with the inevitable sparkling blue waters of Waitemata Harbour in view. Green pot plants lined the length of the window.

Entranced, Cindy could only stare, barely hearing the receptionist announce her or leave the office. Though she soon came back down to earth with a thump, as the large man turned from his position at the window, his hands in his trouser pockets and his stance casual.

'Well, well, Cindy Taylor, so we *do* meet again — and so soon,' his voice drawled.

Shock barely registered. All Cindy experienced was a sudden need to escape. Calmly turning on her heel, she strode over to the door, her mind completely blank but her reflexes alive, urging her to flee.

But Stuart Newman was too quick for her and was standing in front of the door by the time she reached it, forcing her to stop. She looked up at him coldly.

'Where are you going? Have you forgotten what you came here for?' he asked, his eyes alight with amusement.

'I've changed my mind.'

'What about?'

'About working here.'

'I don't really remember offering you the position.' He wrinkled his brow and rubbed his chin with his hand, his eyes still amused.

Cindy went rigid. He was getting the better of her, but then he was the type that always would get the better of people, a man who would tie a person up in

27

knots before they realized what was happening. To save herself any embarrassment she decided that it would be wiser to refrain from answering him back. 'Please let me pass.'

'Certainly not. I've remained here in my office for the express purpose of this interview. I'm not wasting my time just because you suddenly get cold feet. You need a job, I take it?'

'Yes, but I'm not desperate enough to have to take a job from you,' Cindy snapped.

'Honey, right now jobs are rather hard to come by, so if you want to be stuck behind some shop counter or work in a factory then you're going the right way about it. I seem to recall gaining the impression that you were looking for a job out of the ordinary, with spice and adventure. That right?'

'That's right, but not what you have in mind.'

Stuart's expression grew cold. 'I have no intention of chasing you around my desk or forcing you to sit on my knee to take dictation. If you worked for me then you'd work — and damn hard.

'You're nothing but a kid, and just because I felt like a bit of amusement that Friday night you needn't get any big ideas that I wish to carry on where I left off. I don't usually indulge in trying to make advances to babies, so you can pretend that Friday's unfortunate incident had never been — okay? Now sit down.' He threw a pencil and pad on to the top of his desk and motioned her to sit down. Walking over to resume his position facing the window he began dictating rapidly.

As there was not much else for it, Cindy sat down and reached for the pad and pencil and took down what he was saying in shorthand.

'Did you get that down?' he asked at length.

'Ye-es, I think so.' At his abrupt order she read it back, haltingly at first, then with growing confidence.

Stuart nodded and sat down behind his desk and

began to explain to her just exactly what the job entailed and what would be expected of her. 'The staff of the hotel are entitled to concession rates in hotels throughout New Zealand. Sometime this year or early next year I intend to travel to Australia to open a hotel in Sydney. I'll expect my secretary to be able to accompany me. There will be other trips later on to the Cook Islands, perhaps Fiji and others throughout New Zealand, for all of which I'll need a secretary, so it would be necessary for her to have no attachments. Does travelling sound adventurous enough for you?'

Wide-eyed, Cindy nodded, rapidly forgetting her distrust of this man, her mind's eye picturing what Stuart was telling her. Sydney, Australia! Auckland was big, but Sydney . . .

'You needn't look like that,' Stuart told her grimly. 'They won't be pleasure trips. There'll be work, work and more work. You'll be lucky to even catch a glimpse of either Bondi or Manly Beaches in Sydney.' He went on to fill her in on the other details such as salary, holidays and sick leave, etcetera. 'Well?' he said finally, 'what do you think?'

'Are — are you offering *me* the job?'

'Well, you did apply with the hope of getting it, didn't you?' he snapped irritably.

'Yes — but I have had no previous office experience.'

'No, but I think you have a willingness to work which is often hard to find,' he told her, lifting the receiver of the grey telephone ringing insistently on his desk.

He rummaged around in his drawer and found a form and pen and motioned her to fill it in as he spoke in curt monosyllables to the person on the other end of the line.

Hesitantly, Cindy completed the form. 'Why?' she asked herself. 'Why me? Surely there were other appli-

29

cants much more efficient and experienced than I am and who also have a willingness to work. And do I want the job? Sure, it's a great chance and a good job and one I'll enjoy, but with Stuart Newman as my boss?' Cindy stared at him openly.

He was hard, as hard as granite, ruthless and cruel. Cindy could tell by the purposeful way in which he did most things, a way that wasn't to be thwarted. Pity help anyone who stood in his way, she thought.

His face, rugged almost to the point of ugliness, was rather screw-off in that it looked as though his jaw might have been broken at one time — perhaps while playing rugby. He had a long mouth, thin except for a slightly fuller lower lip. His nose, too, looked like it had been broken once or even twice. In fact the only feature that stopped him from being devilish ugly was his eyes, dark, thickly fringed and widely spaced under thick black brows, which instead gave him an appearance of being devilishly attractive, but also world-weary and disillusioned.

Suddenly he glanced up and caught her unawares, staring at him. Hastily she lowered her gaze and scribbled her signature on the bottom of the form and dotted the full-stop with a thud of finality.

Stuart's lean long-fingered hand drew it to him, scanning it he looked up and nodded and waved her away with his hand. 'Tomorrow at nine,' he mouthed to her, and turned his attention back to what the person was saying to him on the telephone.

'Well, there's no use in haggling over the whys and buts,' she told herself as she went out into the warm winter sun which made Auckland's climate so popular. 'I've committed myself now. Whether it's for better or for worse I'll no doubt find out soon.'

However, she still couldn't shake the suspicion that this whole interview had been foreseen; that Stuart Newman had been expecting her even before she had rang through to make her appointment.

She felt happier though, and rather proud of herself as she stood outside of her cousin's home and looked down at Mission Bay, a blue crescent of sea resting in a long and curving white arm of sand which in turn ran beside a wide border of green parade.

'Only one of Auckland's million and one beauty spots,' she thought, 'and I have yet a million others to see.'

She was in the city now. A beautiful modern city, sprawling over mountainous hills and extinct volcanoes, around glorious bays and wide stretches of deep blue sea and all in a warm tropical climate for the best part of the year, despite the winter, and surrounded by tropical scenery with snow-capped mountains, tangled bush country and farming areas less than a few hours' drive away.

'All this and a job which most girls would envy. What more could anyone ask?' Cindy thought contentedly and went on up to the house. Her life was only just beginning, but in what form it was to take she had yet to discover.

Cindy decided to make her announcement when they were all seated at the table for dinner. She wanted to choose her moment, for she knew that her cousin, Jo, would be as thrilled, if not more so, about her success as she was herself. Keith would be pleased too of course, though only in a quiet, kindly sort of way. But Jo, being a highly successful decorator, basically a business-minded woman, would know what it meant to be able to settle into a good position first off, with excellent prospects and opportunities.

As Cindy studied her cousin across the table she realized that she was going through rather a sad and happy period. Sad because in a short time she would be forced to give up the job she loved so much and happy because she had another new position to look forward to — motherhood. 'But,' she had hastened to assure Cindy, 'I won't be leaving the world of decorating altogether. I'll have tons of time to really get stuck into redecorating this place. I've done part of it as you can see, but I just can't find the time to really get into it. The week-ends just aren't long enough.'

At that moment Jo looked up to catch Cindy's eyes upon her and smiled at her. 'Do anything exciting today?'

'Yes,' Cindy was delighted at the wonderful opening Jo had unwittingly put forward. 'I found myself a job.'

'You've what?'

'I've got myself a job,' Cindy announced, picking up her knife and fork and began cutting the gravy-covered meat on her plate.

'Well, that was rather sudden, wasn't it? — but exciting. Whereabouts?'

'The Southern Cross Hotel, as secretary to the Hotelier, and I'll be starting tomorrow.' With eager enthusiasm she explained what had happened earlier that afternoon and the prospects and wonderful opportunities the position offered.

However, her voice trailed off as she became conscious of the sudden pallor of Jo's face and the tenseness in Keith's. There was silence for a moment before Cindy exclaimed: 'What on earth's the matter? I thought you two would be pleased, but instead you both sit there like two petrified mummies.'

'Stuart Newman,' was all Jo said.

'Why, yes — how did you know?'

Jo gave a mirthless laugh. 'Oh, I know Stuart Newman all right. There are not many girls who don't know or meet a Stuart Newman at one time or another.'

'What do you mean?' Cindy asked bewilderedly, looking from Jo to Keith.

'I think what Jo means is that she — that we both

think that deciding to work for Stuart Newman would be an unwise decision,' Keith told her quietly.

Cindy remained silent for a moment, her heart contracting in sudden fear. 'I still don't understand.'

'Well, I don't quite know how to put this, but I don't think he is the sort of boss a young inexperienced girl like you should have . . .' Jo began.

'Oh, for heaven's sake!' Cindy interrupted impatiently, her fear and puzzlement, not to mention her disappointment at this unforeseen reaction to her exciting news, putting an edge to her temper. 'Give it to me straight. I'm twenty — not a child any longer.'

'All right then,' Jo's voice strengthened with unconcealed loathing as she went on. 'Stuart Newman is nothing but a swine. He's bad, Cindy, and will stop at nothing to get what he wants. He's ruthless and cruel.'

Cindy's blood chilled at her cousin's words. Were her own suspicions correct after all?

'And conquering women is one of his major achievements and he wallows in his victories and gloats over them. He breaks a woman like he would break a twig — by snapping it between his fingers — and he'll probably break you if you don't keep out of his way. He has no scruples or conscience and he actually enjoys it. You're young, untried, but that won't stop him . . .'

'You speak as though — as though you know him,' Cindy shivered. There was silence while Jo and Keith glanced at each other. 'How do you know?'

Keith spoke first. 'Jo had a very good friend called Anne. She saw what happened to her. You'll just have to trust us.'

Jo nodded in agreement with Keith. 'Please trust us and take our word for it. Clear out before it's too late. Don't learn through your own mistakes. Please, Cindy, be sensible.'

Dumbly, Cindy looked at her, hearing her pleading voice with sincerity underlining every word. Leave her job — before she had even started. Leave Stuart Newman before it was too late. But something was holding her back. Could it already be too late? Panic moved her. Of course it wasn't too late. 'I could never see him again and it wouldn't worry me,' she told herself. But involuntarily she remembered the feel of his hard, cold lips on the skin of her neck and shoulders and laughing breath on her mouth.

She thrust the memory aside. It was the job she wanted. Stuart Newman wasn't the attraction. Why, she thoroughly disliked him as a person, so Jo and Keith's advice wasn't really necessary where she was concerned.

'Cindy, listen to me. Give up the job. There are others. I don't want to see you hurt or degraded. You will be if you remain in Stuart Newman's hands.'

It was clear that, by Jo's pleading, her friend must have suffered a great deal in those ruthless hands. However, Cindy shook her head.

'You won't give it up?'

'No, Jo, I'm sorry, but the job is a good one. Too good to miss. Don't worry, I can take care of myself.'

'There is no such sentence when speaking of someone like Stuart Newman. He's like a charming devil. When in his company a girl doesn't want to be capable of taking care of herself.'

After getting ready for bed that night, Jo sat down in front of her dressing table mirror and stared at her reflection.

She turned and smiled fondly, but a little worriedly, at her husband, as if she needed some words of encouragement and reassurance which he gave. 'She'll be all right, honey. As she said, she knows how to take care of herself.'

'Yes, but then I thought I did too,' Jo sighed.

Cindy started work the next morning, nervous and

apprehensive. Jo's words were still repeating themselves in her brain and no matter how much she tried to ignore them they still succeeded in planting seeds of doubt in her mind.

She wouldn't give up this job, but she would be extra wary. She was determined that nothing would induce her to fall susceptible to Stuart Newman's charm like so many before her. 'After all, forewarned is forearmed, and I have been warned,' she thought, brushing aside the realization that she had suspected Stuart for what he was at their first meeting and if she had, a mere country girl, surely the others before her had. The realization was a somehow frightening one.

She had entered the front entrance of the Southern Cross Hotel when again she was visited by a familiar urge to escape, turn and run. But no, she quickened her step. She wasn't going to give Stuart the satisfaction of knowing that she had backed down and bolted like a scared rabbit, and by his first sentence she was glad she hadn't.

'So, Cindy Taylor, you didn't back out after all,' Stuart's sarcastic voice greeted her as she entered his office.

It was on the tip of her tongue to retort that she had been advised to, but said instead: 'No, why should I? I have got myself a good job with wonderful opportunities.'

'And a wonderful boss?' he mocked.

'There are always disadvantages with every job, Mr. Newman. I'm willing to take the good with the bad.' 'Blow him,' she thought, to herself, 'I can give as good as he can. At least I've learned how to out in the backblocks and I intend to.'

'Well, then, that I'm glad to hear.' He had deliberately misinterpreted her meaning.

'If he keeps rubbing me up the wrong way like this, then Jo need have no fear that I'll fall for him in any way.' She stood holding his lazy regard expressionlessly.

He nodded and stood up. 'Right. Come and I'll introduce you to Sue Randal, one of our receptionists. She'll show you around and introduce you to various members of the staff.'

Sue Randal was a friendly girl who had a bright and cheerful personality which had probably got her her job as one of the hotel's receptionists. She showed Cindy around the exclusive hotel, introducing her to different people, staff and patrons alike.

'I suppose you get to see and meet a lot of interesting people?' Cindy remarked after having been introduced to an American couple who, Sue informed her, were touring around New Zealand at their own leisure.

'Yeah, but I'd give it all up to be in your shoes right now,' Sue eyed her enviously.

'Yes, I am looking forward to travelling around. I'm glad to have a job which gives me the chance to be able to,' Cindy said.

Sue looked at her, a dumbfounded expression on her face. 'Say, are you for real?'

'What do you mean?'

'I'll tell you what I didn't mean and that was all those free trips you'll be getting. I'm talking about Mr. Newman, you know, your boss. Don't tell me you haven't noticed the hotel's No. One heart-throb?'

'Oh — oh, of course,' Cindy laughed. 'I didn't think for a moment that was what you were getting at,' she added truthfully.

'You'll discover that he is all that people do remark on around here. No go though.' Sue pulled down the corners of her mouth and gestured flatly. 'He doesn't associate with members of his staff. Not in that way unfortunately. Against the rules.'

'Funny,' Cindy murmured unthinkingly. 'I didn't

think he would be the type to let an opportunity pass and certainly not to make a point of ruling it out.'

'Oh, so you have noticed then,' Sue said craftily. 'Don't worry, if you fall for him you can join the Club. Everyone here is nuts about him. He needn't pay us a cent but we would all work for him for nothing.'

'Don't you worry. I have not the slightest intention of falling for him. I don't even like him over much.'

'Time will tell. That was the fate of his other secretary and he calmly asked her to leave. Poor thing. But even he is human, believe it or not. He fell in love with a woman, Delia someone, and boy, was she a cool customer . . .'

'Please, Sue, I'd rather you didn't tell me. It seems that everyone in Auckland has met up with him sometime or another and no one has anything good to say about him so I'd rather not hear it. I'll probably learn myself in time.'

'Okay,' Sue shrugged. 'Tell me, are you living in or flatting?'

'Neither. I'm boarding with my cousin and her husband.'

'I see. Well, I was just going to assure you that the facilities are very good if you're living in. Most of the Aussie girls here on working holidays find it a wonderful save on their funds. Well, back to the grindstone,' she ended merrily when they were standing outside Stuart Newman's office once more. 'Give me a buzz on the phone if you want to know anything, won't you?'

Cindy's first two days at the Southern Cross Hotel were relatively lax ones where work was concerned. She met almost every member of the staff before the days were through and had only typed a few pages of copy typing, some letters and ran a few messages.

Stuart was as good as his word and didn't chase her around the office or force her on to his lap to take down his dictation. In fact at times Cindy was certain that he wasn't even aware of her existence and, when he was, he merely sized her up with a lazy glance behind narrowed lids, a glance which had the power to turn her skin hot and set her pulses leaping.

She was glad when it was at last time to go home. It was clear to her that she was going to have to accept Stuart Newman as he was and getting used to him as being an attractive, but unattainable boss and ruthless and disturbing man, wasn't going to be as easy as she had first thought.

On Saturday, Cindy stood at the doorway and surveyed the room which was to be the baby's bedroom. Jo had just finished decorating it in colours of blue, with cherry drapes at the windows and rug which lay on the carpeted floor.

Wallpaper with Disney characters painted all over it covered one of the walls and a huge transfer of Mickey Mouse and one of Bambi were fixed to each end of the baby's cot.

'Well, how do you like it?' Jo asked when Cindy went back to the kitchen to help prepare lunch.

'It's lovely, and the colours are gorgeous,' Cindy enthused. 'You must have gone to a lot of bother doing it.'

'I loved every minute of it, although I tend to tire more easily now which is a nuisance.' She sighed. 'But I suppose it will all be worth it.'

'Of course it will!' Cindy assured her with a smile. 'Going by the colours of the room I'd say you were wanting a boy.'

'Keith wants a boy naturally enough, and I think I'd rather have a boy first.' Jo smiled. 'He's so good to me.' She stared out of the kitchen window at Keith mowing the large expanse of green lawn. 'I'm really lucky. He's a good husband, better than I deserve, and in addition I have everything I could possibly want,' she gestured around the huge kitchen, so up to date and equipped with every convenience. It was a bright kitchen with many wide venetian blind-covered windows which let in both the morning and afternoon sun. 'Oh, I know many married couples today have just about everything that opens and shuts, but not a beautiful home such as this, in a beautiful area and so near the sea.'

'Of course you deserve it, and more,' Cindy retorted.

'Oh, honey,' Josh took her head, 'you don't know, you just don't know. Still, I'd better not sink into the doldrums. Guess what my wonderful husband has planned for us tonight?' She cut up the lettuce with quick deft movements and placed the shreds into a bowl and began to grate carrots over the top.

'I don't know. What?'

'We're all going out for dinner tonight. To the new Norfolk Restaurant at Remuera, and then to the movies.'

'How lovely, but wouldn't you rather go out by yourselves.'

'Certainly not. When the baby comes — perhaps then I'll accept your offer to stay behind and babysit,' Jo threw her a wink. 'Don't be too fussy about slicing those, they are only going to get eaten,' she added as she saw Cindy take up the knife to slice the tomatoes and hard boiled eggs.

In readiness for dining out that night, Cindy dressed in an ice blue frock, fitting, with a wide scooped neckline and blue crystal beads sewn over the bodice. She wore silver sandals and bag and her best coat, a smokey grey-blue one made of soft fur fabric. It had cost her the best part of fifty dollars in Palmerston North, a city not far from her home-town, but it suited her admirably and despite her earlier doubts, she was now glad she had bought it. Jo had swept her hair up into a neat swirl on to the back of her head and this, together with her clothes and carefully applied make-up, made her look older and decidedly beautiful.

Jo, too, looked lovely in a lurex threaded green frock with silver beads sewn on to its stand-up collar. The frock did much to hide the fact that she was expecting and the colour suited her warm honey colouring.

And Keith's reaction wasn't at all disappointing. 'Wow! Two beautiful girls, one on each arm. I'll be the envy of the city tonight.'

Jo laughed and hugged his arm to her. 'Now, now, darling. Remember which one is your wife.'

The new restaurant was situated in a secluded spot with tall Norfolk pine trees either side of it. Lights shone softly from windows and terraces and music drifted to them from within.

'It looks fabulous,' Jo murmured appreciatively, taking in every detail of the interior with an artistic eye. The rich vibrant colours appealed to her immensely.

They were shown to their table by the waiter and sat down to study the menu.

'Heavens, what to decide!' Cindy remarked.

'Have something out of the ordinary, something you don't get at home,' Keith told her.

'Then what if I don't like it?'

'I'll eat it,' he grinned.

Cindy laughed. 'Brilliant!' Suddenly the laughter was choked out of her as her gaze drifted beyond Keith to two men sitting at another table not far from them. In the pale light her gaze met the dark eyes of Stuart Newman.

'That's what he wants you to do, so take no notice of him,' Jo was saying, but Cindy didn't hear her. The loud thud of her heart was blocking out everything, even the music.

Stuart was reclining back in his chair, slowly and deliberately taking in every detail of her appearance.

From her upswept hair to her darkened eyelids and lashes, her eyes to the creamy base of her throat and the low-necked sparkly dress. She actually felt his eyes caressing her bare neck and shoulders and slender arms.

So personal was his observation, she was almost sure that he could see the pulse beating at her throat. She tensed in anger. 'How dare he look me over like that!' She stared at him coldly. He made no effort to lift a hand acknowledging that he recognized her and neither did he smile a greeting.

'He just looks me up and down like he would any other girl he considered worth his attention and in that case the girl would probably give the "Come hither" look, thinking that he was genuinely interested, either that or not caring one way or the other whether he was or not,' Cindy thought, and casting him a final icy stare, she turned her attention back to Jo and Keith. If he was going to ignore her then it was all right by her. She was only too willing to try and spare Jo the knowledge of his presence if she could.

They finished their dinner during which Cindy didn't look over at Stuart again, but laughed and joked with Jo and Keith. So engrossed was she in her effort to forget Stuart, she didn't see him approach their table and wasn't aware of him until he was actually standing beside her.

'Good evening, Cindy.'

She looked up, startled, and saw his amused eyes mocking her.

'Hello, Jo, Keith.' He held out his hand to Keith who ignored it.

Concernedly, Cindy looked at Jo who sat tense, but poised. She had paled noticeably, but her hardened gaze didn't falter from his. 'Good evening, Stuart. This is a coincidence.'

'Yes, isn't it? How are you keeping?'

'Fine, thank you, and you?'

'Just fine,' Stuart nodded and turned to Cindy. 'I hate to mix business with pleasure, but I won't be in the office on Monday until after lunch so I'd like you to make all appointments for the afternoon — okay?'

Cindy nodded, not daring to speak in case her voice should be as shaky as her hands.

'Would you like to dance? The band has started up quite a beat,' he said with a lazy smile.

Didn't he have any shame? Didn't he care that both Keith and Jo are treating him as coldly off-putting as a place like this allowed? Didn't he feel the least bit uncomfortable? Cindy wondered. She shook her head. 'No — no, thank you, I don't think there'll be time,' she answered, looking at Keith.

'She's right,' Keith nodded, getting to his feet and Jo following suit. He glanced down at his watch. 'We're going to the movies so we'll have to get cracking.'

'It's been so nice seeing you again, Stuart,' Jo smiled and turned to follow her husband towards the door. There had been a sneer in her voice and smile which surprised Cindy. Jo was always so sweet that she didn't think she was capable of any such felinity.

Murmuring a hurried: 'Goodnight, Mr. Newman,' Cindy gathered up her coat and handbag and Stuart watched as she quickly left the restaurant and then turned back to rejoin his friend.

'Wasn't that Jo Dixon?' Paul Brent asked as Stuart sat down.

'Yeah, though she's Mrs. Jo Morrison now.'

Paul raised an eyebrow. 'Really? And who is the gorgeous young chick with her?'

'My new secretary.'

'Fair go?' Paul laughed in surprise. 'She's a beauty,

but a bit young, isn't she, or have your tastes changed?'

'Maybe.'

'Come on, give. Have you got her eating out of your hand yet? It usually doesn't take you long.'

'You forget that there is a rule at the hotel.'

'That doesn't mean to say that if the opportunity is offering you wouldn't take it — and she looks really delectable.'

'She is — an innocent young thing from the back-blocks. And I haven't got her eating out of my hand because she doesn't go for that sort of thing. She has set high ideals and so far has lived up to them.'

Paul looked taken aback at this. 'Surely you can do better than that, Stuart. It doesn't matter how high their ideals are, one look at you and they fall, hook, line and sinker — why, I don't know, you're about as ugly as Satan himself. Anyway, what's stopping you exerting that renowned charm? You're not usually as slow as this.'

'I have made a bargain with my housekeeper.'

'Who, Elizabeth?'

Stuart nodded. 'I took Cindy home to my house, soaking wet and shivering like a cold, wet rabbit ready to bolt with fright. Elizabeth, I think, took pity on her and gave me a sound lecture until I felt bound to give my word not to lead her on like she thought I would, the rat I am.'

'And you promised her that?' Paul asked, astounded.

'More-or-less.'

'What do you mean, more-or-less?'

'I promised her that I wouldn't let her get too deeply involved with me.' Stuart flicked his lighter and set the flame to his cigarette and watched the smoke rise up into the already smoke-filled atmosphere.

Paul laughed. 'You're a rat all right, a cunning one. Quite a challenge, eh?'

'What the hell do you mean?'

'Well, don't tell me you hadn't thought of changing the young thing's mind?'

'Like hell,' Stuart lied. 'She's proving a good secretary. I don't want to lose her.'

'Why not? Get a conscientious old war horse who will keep the lovelorn at bay. Or could it be you've already tried changing her mind only to find that our young secretary doesn't take to you?' Paul added shrewdly.

Stuart's eyes narrowed, holding his. He laughed. 'She's fighting it and hates my guts.'

'Aha, so now we get the real truth. What do you plan to do about it?'

Stuart shrugged. 'Plenty of time. Right now she's a good secretary.'

'No, there's not plenty of time.'

Stuart crushed out his cigarette. 'What are you getting at.'

'I bet you can't get her to fall for you inside a month.'

'Don't be silly.'

'I don't mean just the "secretary falls for her boss" bit. I mean the real thing, but, so that you keep your promise to Elizabeth. What's the date? June, 20th. Right, you've got until July 20th to conquer your respectable, backblock secretary. How about it?'

'You know, I thought I was the fink around here, but you're catching up, Brent, fast. How much do you bet?' Stuart's face took on a hard expression, the one of a ruthless man.

'Forty dollars.'

'Are you putting me on? That won't even keep me in cigarettes. It's a tough assignment, tougher than it looks.'

'Okay, my stag head, you know that twelve-pointer you've always wanted.'

There was a pause during which Stuart eyed his friend in disgust. 'You double-crossing . . . you've promised me that head ever since you shot it, and now I have to accomplish the almost impossible to get it!'

'Not the impossible, Newman. And I know I promised to give it to you but I changed my mind. I knew, if I kept it long enough, I'd be able to bribe you of something one day, and if you lose I'm still keeping it, so keep that in mind. I know it was I who shot it but you still want it to hang in that ranch type house of yours.'

Stuart whistled angrily through his teeth.

'Is it a deal?'

'It's a deal. And if I lose then we're both going to take time out to go shooting and neither of us is going to emerge from that bush until my bullet finds me a stag with an even twelve-point antler, even if we have to comb the North and South Islands. Okay?' Stuart stood up.

Paul let out a whoop of delight and, keeping his cigarette clenched between his teeth, he got to his feet and searched for his wallet. Slamming some money on to the table, he slapped Stuart on his back. 'Too right it's okay, and it's okay by me if we stay in that bush forever. Just imagine it, fishing, shooting and hunting the rest of our lives. Cooking fish and boar over open fires, putting up in those god-forsaken huts, hunting along the banks of the Wanganui, climbing the mountains. Just picture it, Newman, just picture it.'

'I am, buddy boy, I am, but don't count on it. I intend winning my bet.'

Paul shook his head. 'I'm not counting on anything, pal, not even on you winning that bet.'

CHAPTER THREE

BY FIVE-THIRTY on Monday, rain was pelting down from low-hanging black clouds and winds were buffeting people about like helpless dummies. To make matters worse, Cindy, having to remain behind a fraction longer than usual, to change her shoes to waterproof boots and buckle up her rain coat and make an unsuccessful attempt to push her hair up under a rain hat, had missed her bus.

'Oh, a thousand and one — damns!' Cindy muttered. She kicked through a puddle and watched as the water splashed up on to her shiny coat and sprang into tiny sparkling bubbles on the resistant material, then grimaced as the remainder of the water dribbled down inside her boots.

She listened to the cars speed past her as she walked along to the nearest taxi stand, not far from the Hotel. Their rubber tyres hissed on the wet surface, horns honked impatiently and brakes squealed as the five-thirty homegoers broke all records in an endeavour to escape the heavy traffic.

'I'll never get a taxi,' Cindy groaned, as waiting people piled into the taxis lined up against the kerb. Fed up, she slipped into a nearby telephone booth and rang Jo.

'Hi, Jo, it's me, Cindy. I'm sorry but I may be a little late. I've just missed my bus and the taxis are getting snapped up as fast as they come in. I'm sorry to be such a nuisance.'

'Don't be silly, I know it can be terribly frustrating waiting for taxis in the rain. Look, I'll get Keith to pick you up. He should be home any minute.'

'No — no, don't put him to any trouble. I just

thought I'd better let you know where I've got to in case you started worrying.'

'Okay then, but don't wait too long in the rain. Keith won't mind picking you up.'

Cindy rang off and went out into the thickly falling rain, her eyes squinting at the sudden brightness of oncoming car lights. Temporarily blinded, she walked straight into an advancing figure of a man. 'Oops!'

Two hands shot out to grasp her arms to stop her from falling backwards. Furiously, Cindy pushed back her hat which had slipped over her eyes and glared up at the man, bareheaded and smiling.

Stuart Newman! Surprise made her loosen her hold on her hat and in a sudden gust of wind she felt it being lifted from her head. 'Oh, my hat!' she cried, and started to run after it as it whirled down the street along its brim, but was stopped by Stuart's hand tightening on her arm.

'Leave it. You'll never get it back in this. I'll get you a new one — come to think of it I owe you a new dress.'

'But my hat — it matches my coat!' Cindy protested tearfully, struggling for an upright position after Stuart had very nearly swung her off her feet.

Stuart shrugged. 'So what? I'll get you a new coat. Come on, get into my car, it's parked up here further, before you get soaked to the skin again. I'm sure you're not too keen on another abduction.'

Cindy found herself being thrust into Stuart's black Ford Falcon and felt the suspension sink as he got in beside her, appearing even bigger in his dark overcoat.

He threw her a grin as he started up the car. With rain sparkling on his skin and hair, he looked druggedly attractive. Taken off her guard, Cindy smiled back and Stuart was amazed to feel the impact of her smile as it struck him it was the first real smile she had given him.

'What the devil were you doing wandering around in this? Don't you usually catch a bus,' he asked, 'or do you just like the rain? Every time I see you, you seem to be splashing around in it.'

'I like it, but not so much that I'd walk home in it. I missed my bus.'

'Ah yes, you're living with your cousin now, eh? Jo Morrison. She was Jo Dixon when I knew her.'

'Yes.' Cindy stiffened, once more on her guard.

'Well, well, it's a small world. Where to, by the way?'

Cindy told him Jo's address.

He grimaced. 'Done pretty well for herself.'

Cindy frowned. What was he trying to imply by that remark? 'What do you mean?'

He cast her a swift sideways glance. 'Are you kidding?' it seemed to say. 'What does Jo think of you working for me? Surely she warned you against me — what I've done and what I'm like?'

'She did, but I decide for myself.'

Just as Stuart was going to mentally chalk that down as one in his favour, she continued: 'It was the job that attracted me — not the boss.'

He laughed grimly. 'As I said — a smart cookie. I still don't understand it. Surely she laid it on thick enough to make you want even a house cleaning job?'

Cindy felt puzzled. She was about to say: 'It's none of my business about what happened between you and her best friend,' but he went on: 'I can't believe two cousins can be so different — and I don't mean in looks.'

'Mr. Newman, I can't grasp what you're trying to imply.'

'Well, it goes without saying, you, so innocent and untouched, so pure in your convictions, so entirely opposite to your cousin. It's amazing.' He spoke sarcastically.

'I think you'd better stop where you are, Mr. Newman,' Cindy said. 'Being my employer doesn't give you the right to talk down on my relatives. My cousin . . .'

'Look, honey, that doesn't alter the fact that she is what she is. Innocent though you are, you must be grown up enough to realize that just because she's your cousin it doesn't automatically stop her from being the sort of girl she is!'

The hard, coldly spoken insinuation lashed her, making her cry out in protest. 'You — you — rotter! How dare you speak of her in such a way? You're a liar! She's not like that — she's not!'

Stuart looked sideways at her shock-filled face. He pulled the car up at the side of the road, then turned and took her by the shoulders and drew her closer to his menacing face. 'You listen to me you safe, over-protected little prig! You'll grow up one day and you'll also learn what it is to grow up. You'll learn what people are and what they aren't and you'll have to learn to live with the knowledge that people, no matter how close they are to you or how much they mean to you, are only human and not some dream person you may want them to be and build them up to be. You can't change them and neither can your refusal to face the truth.' He shook her. 'Do you understand that? All right, Jo was in love with me, or she thought she was. She was beautiful and aware of her beauty, she was forward and she knew she was forward, she offered me her beauty and I took it. She knew full well what she was doing, no matter what yarn she may have spun you. So now you know the truth from my angle. She was hard and out for all she could get. Well, she's got it. An infant, a husband and a flash home — and in that order. Whether or not you accept that either from her or from him, it makes no difference, it's what has happened.'

Cindy sat limp against the seat where he flung her, stunned and utterly numb. She watched the wind-screen wipers swish this way and that, not really seeing them, but concentrating on the odd shapes into which the dampness sprang after the wipers had cleared away the rain drops. So curiously like dis-garded tears, the drops ran in rivulets down the sides of the window.

'Who — who is Anne?' she asked, in a voice which one might associate with Alice in her Wonderland.

'Anne who?' Stuart asked between teeth clenched over the cigarette he was lighting.

'Oh — I don't know,' Cindy said in that same voice. 'Oh, Keith told me about her — and you — the two of you. They warned me about you because you had hurt Anne so dreadfully. That was all they told me. Jo didn't tell me about her and you — or the baby.'

There was complete silence within the car. Bluish smoke swirled around them and Cindy put up her hand to wave it away from the front of her face. Suddenly she was jerked around by Stuart's steely ruthless hands on her arms.

'She didn't tell you?' he demanded.

The feel of his hands on her, so strong and non-slackening, suddenly made the full shock of what he had just told her hit her. Hate for him burned through her so fierily that she frightened herself. Never had she experienced this emotion over anyone before.

'Take your hands off me!' she gritted through her teeth. She squirmed in his hold. 'You damn liar — let me go! You're a liar — a liar, do you hear me?' Sobs racked through her, making her increasingly hysterical as well as breathless.

In a sharp movement he brought his hand up and hit her hard across the side of her face. Dazed, she stared at him through strands of hair which had fallen over her face, his own was almost invisible in the blackness of the shadows. Then tears began to rivulet down her cheeks like those on the windscreen of the car.

'I am sorry,' Stuart said expressionlessly when her sobs had quietened. 'It didn't occur to me that you didn't know.'

Wiping the palms of her hands across her cheeks, Cindy sensed that somehow he wasn't really sorry, but in any case it didn't really matter. Even if he was sorry it would make no difference. What was said was said and no apology could alter that. 'Please, just take me home,' she said quietly, staring blankly out of the side window.

Nothing was said during the remaining distance driven to Mission Bay. Stuart brought the car to a halt alongside the kerb and, climbing out, he came around to where Cindy was slowly closing the door. He caught her arm as she was about to pass him unseeingly.

'You once told me I was a cruel man.' He lifted her face to his. 'Look at me!' he commanded curtly. 'Maybe I am cruel in many ways and maybe I have reason to be, but you must believe this — I didn't do and say what I did deliberately. There was nothing to gain. I had no wish to come between you and your cousin.'

Cindy held his gaze. 'You haven't, Mr. Newman. What you have just told me doesn't make me respect my cousin any less, or dislike her, but it does make me pity you. It must be terrible to be so — so unloved and uncared for as you, so utterly alone. Oh yes, you try to hide it under that hard, cynical front you put up, but you feel it and it's obvious, to me, at any rate, that you may be slightly envious of Jo's happiness.'

Stuart stood looking after her for a few seconds before getting back into his car and driving away. His expression was one of profound anger. He was angry with her, and with himself at feeling a strong desire to hit her and not just as a method of putting a stop to hysteria, but because he knew, although he wouldn't admit it, that she, as young as she might be, saw further into him than he cared for.

After she had hung up her coat and removed her boots in the washhouse, Cindy went through to the kitchen where Jo was dishing out the dinner and Keith was sitting reading the evening paper.

'Hi, Cindy. Manage to get a taxi after all?' Jo smiled, looking up from scooping out spoonfuls of mashed potato.

Cindy forced a smile. 'Of a kind.' She filled the hot-water jug and plugged in the cord beside the stove.

'You look pensive, anything the matter?' Jo asked, licking a dob of mashed potato off her knuckle and rinsing the empty pot under the cold water tap.

Cindy shook her head and managed a yawn behind her hand. 'Just tired. It's amazing how days like this can be so depressing. I think I'll have an early night.'

'You must be tired. You seldom miss the Virginian on telly,' Jo laughed, but all the same she didn't fail to notice Cindy's wan colour. 'Are you sure you're feeling okay? Not in for a dose of the 'flu or anything?'

'No, nothing that a good night's sleep won't cure.'

Jo said nothing more. However, she felt sure that there was more to it than Cindy was letting on, and knowing that she was with Stuart Newman all day, every day, caused her extra concern as her imagination persisted to haunt her by conjuring up what possible harm she could come to under his influence.

Cindy went to work the next morning as usual, and automatically drew back the long drapes in both offices, removed the cover from her typewriter, put out the 'ins' and 'outs' trays from her drawers, watered the plants and whipped a yellow duster along the surface of desks, cabinets and window sills.

She heard Stuart arrive and as soon as she had finished opening the mail and sorting it out into their correct piles she took it into him, also taking her shorthand pad and pencil.

'Good morning, Mr. Newman,' she said, her tone devoid of its customary cheerfulness.

'Morning, Cindy.' He looked up at her.

'I've sorted out the mail. These, I think, are personal so I've left them unopened. Reservations, accounts and receipts etcetera and the others are general business. If you like, I'll take this lot to their respective departments before taking dictation.'

'No — no, I've got rather an urgent letter on my mind, so I'd rather it got sent off right away.'

'Very well.'

From his usual position at the window, he watched her sit down and open her note book, her pencil poised over it. 'She has changed,' he found himself thinking. 'Almost overnight. She seems to have got older, more drawn into herself.'

He was sorry about what had happened the night before and this surprised him, for he seldom felt sorry for anything he did. In fact, just the opposite when he succeeded in hitting back at the fair sex. Perhaps it was because whatever he did seldom backfired or reacted like last night's episode. It was clear too, that she wanted to forget it, for she was deliberately avoiding the opportunity of broaching the subject, so thinking it wiser he said nothing.

The cool relationship between them lasted out the week, with neither speaking to the other unless it was in regard to business.

Finally, on Friday, Stuart, remembering his bet with Paul Brent, decided that this attitude was getting him nowhere fast. A whole week had gone and he now had only three weeks left in which to endeavour to win his bet and secure ownership of that stag head.

It was a magnificent head. He had been quite envious when it had been Paul and not he who had managed to hunt it down in the South Island bush country — and after he had already informed Paul of his ambition to shoot himself a stag with an even twelve-point antler to display in his home, knowing that it would suit the house and also knowing that an even twelve-pointer was not too easy to come by. As he thought of the prize he became more and more determined to possess it. He gave no further thought to Cindy's personal feelings. She was lucky. He seldom gave thought to anyone's feelings and certainly not those of a treacherous female.

'There you are, the mail ready for your signature.' Cindy came in and set a pile of neatly typed letters on his desk. 'Where do you want me to put these copies you asked me to type?'

'Just leave them on my desk. I'll see to them. You can file these green copies though.' He handed her two sheets of typed paper and watched as she punched holes into the tops and deftly clipped them on to the files in his cabinet.

'Well, another week finished. How are you finding the work?'

'I like it well enough, Mr. Newman.'

He nodded, finished signing the letters and let her fold them and put them into their respective envelopes.

'Are you expected home early tonight?' he asked.

'No, I'm staying in town to do some shopping.'

'Alone?'

'Yes, Mr. Newman.'

Stuart began to feel exasperated with her monotonous cool manner and curt 'Yes, Mr. Newmans' and

'No, Mr. Newmans'. Had it not been for the bet he wouldn't have said any more. He wasn't in the mood for her prudish behaviour and vacant stares. 'Then how about accompanying me to dinner? Elizabeth is away for a week or two and I don't feel much like cooking dinner.' That much was true anyway. All he wanted to do was to have a quiet meal alone, go home, have a hot shower and drop straight into bed. 'Lord, I must be getting old,' he thought. However, he was unprepared for her answer, for he just wasn't use to be getting told 'No'.

'No, thank you, Mr. Newman. Do you want me to post the mail? I'll be going past the P.O., or would you rather do it yourself?'

Then Stuart gave vent to his exasperation. Bringing his fist down on the glass topped table with a crash, he stood up and glowered down at her. A grim smile pulled at his lips as he saw her blink and back away a step. 'To hell with the mail! Look, Miss Smug, Prudence and Virtue, I'm fed up to the teeth with you and the ridiculous way you're going on. I've put up with it and played along with you for the last week and I'm damn sure that I'm not going through another week of it. Now you listen to me, I told you a few home truths about your cousin — I blundered and I apologized. Right? And what happens? For a week I've received the glacial treatment. I thought I employed a responsible young lady as my secretary and instead I find that I've lumbered myself with a stupid child who doesn't even know the time of day. Either you grow up and quit this farce of yours — or quit this job!'

Then something between them seemed to snap and Cindy came back to being herself in one flying instant. She banged the letters down on the desk. 'This job is a farce — the only one I'm playing!' she flared.

'If that's the way you feel then you can still quit!' he retorted thunderously. However, within himself he was exultant. Success! Cindy Taylor was resuming her normal self. A slight start — but nevertheless a start — an important one. Now to start winning his bet.

'Just because I won't have dinner with you,' Cindy sneered. 'My, my — I thought you usually sacked your secretaries because they were all too eager to have dinner with you.'

Stuart leaned back against his desk and folded his arms. 'Oh, and who told you that? One of my over-talkative employees no doubt. Well?'

'Why should I provide the answer? You seem to know them all!' Cindy snapped.

Stuart smiled, a self-satisfied smile. 'I only fire my secretaries when they fancy themselves in love with me — and make it embarrassingly obvious. I'm pleased to know that you value your job as much.'

Cindy caught his meaning. 'Of all the conceited men I've ever met! I'd never fall in love with you if you were the last man on this earth!'

'Prove a cliché true then and dine with me.'

'I don't happen to want to dine with a self-opinionated bore. Do you blame me?'

He held her gaze for a few moments and then inspected his watch. 'According to my watch, it's five o'clock. You don't knock off until five-thirty. So seeing that you are still working for me right now, I would like you to dine with me.'

'I see, Mr. Newman. I didn't think that such a heart-throb had to resort to such lengths to get a dinner date. Still, I'll remember this when you want me to work overtime and you'll know what the answer will be.'

Stuart shrugged. 'I just don't happen to want to dine alone.'

'And you're a man who always gets what he wants!' Cindy finished for him.

'Always.' He whispered the word against her ear as he helped her on with her coat.

She jerked away from him. 'Kindly remember that I'm still your secretary until five-thirty so also remember that I'm entitled to the respect one should expect from an employer.'

He grinned. 'You can go at five-thirty — providing you still want to.'

'On the dot of five-thirty,' Cindy said sharply, and turned on her heel leaving him to follow with the mail.

Stuart stopped outside a small clean restaurant called The Nicoberg. It possessed a dim romantic interior which straight away made Cindy cautious.

'I don't like it!' she stated emphatically at the entrance.

'Why not? It's clean and the food is excellent,' Stuart said innocently. He slipped an arm around her waist and led her towards the approaching waiter.

She stiffened and hissed at him: 'Take your arm away from me!'

He merely smiled at the waiter and tightened his fingers at her waist and tickled her by poking her ribs. 'Table for two,' Stuart told the waiter in a way that made Cindy madder than ever.

Bringing up her hand she placed it on his at her waist. Slowly and deliberately she dug her nails into his flesh, hard.

'Little spitfire, aren't you?' He still didn't relinquish his hold. 'You're going to pay for that, honey.'

'Let go! You have no right to touch me!'

'And if you are a lady, then you had no right to scratch.'

As the waiter led them towards a dark, secluded corner to a table for two, Cindy had a shrewd suspicion that this wasn't the first time Stuart had brought a lady here and that he knew the waiter.

'What would you like?' Stuart asked.

'I'm not sure that I want anything. It's so dark in here I won't be able to see what I'm eating.'

Stuart grinned. 'Well, do you want the candle lit —
to give us a cosy, romantic atmosphere?' he said,
holding the flame of his lighter to the wick.

'Do you think we need it?' Cindy asked sweetly.

'Who knows, if it was cosier you might thaw out
a little and with a little wine you might even become
romantic.'

'No, that wouldn't be any good.'

'Why?'

'Because that would be a farce. Neither of us would
be sincere.'

'Honey, romance is never sincere. Neither side in
romance is really sincere. It's one of the biggest haves
out.'

'Only according to cynics like you. People like you
who don't care about each other or anyone, or whether
they hurt each other, so it comes easy for you to
pretend.'

'Amen!'

The waiter came to their table and Stuart gave
him the order, not bothering to consult her again.

'Haven't you ever cared for anyone?' Cindy asked
bluntly, after studying his face for a moment.

'Whatever brought this on?'

'I'm sorry. I was just wondering, that's all,' Cindy
said quickly, thinking of that beautiful girl in the
photograph whom she was sure was Delia. 'Tell me
about yourself,' she said. 'I bet you were a dinkum
little hardshot when you were a boy.'

His eyes widened, and he looked at her for a
moment, puzzled. 'Why on earth do you want to know
about my boyhood?'

Cindy shrugged. 'I like hearing of the mischievous
adventures of kids, especially boys.'

Stuart grimaced. 'You make me feel like a grand-
father carrying on about the good old days "When
I was a young lad . . ." '

Cindy laughed and rested her chin on her hand,

her eyes twinkling cheekily. 'Well, if it makes you feel any younger, would you rather I asked you about the women in your life?'

His eyes met hers and he replied lazily, calling her bluff: 'Where do you want me to start?'

She blinked a little uncertainly. 'I was only kidding.'

'Backing out, eh? Afraid of being shocked or of being involved?'

Cindy sobered. 'It has nothing to do with me and take it from me that I never intend to get involved with you or become just another conquest for you to add to your list. Never!'

'Never say never. It's a long time, honey.'

There was a silence as the waiter came back carrying a tray bearing their dinner. Cindy looked down at the dish placed in front of her and eagerly picked up her knife and fork. Seeing the beautifully prepared Hawaiian Steak and all the trimmings, she realized just how hungry she was. Suddenly feeling Stuart's eyes on her, she looked up.

He grinned. 'You know it's gone five-thirty?'

'Really? Well don't worry, it's the food that's keeping me, not your charming company,' she retorted.

His grin widened. 'Tell me about your life out in the backblocks, seeing that life histories seem to be the theme of our conversation.'

Cindy waited until she had finished her mouthful of steak before replying: 'There's nothing very exciting to tell really. My parents own a farm some five miles out from Apiti. They called it Hawai Farm. I was an only child and grew up alone more-or-less, but I was contented. There was plenty to do around the farm. The only other kids I knew were those I went with to the country Primary School. You know, those schools which have about a dozen pupils. Actually there were sixteen at this one. Mostly boys, but it didn't matter much for the girls were just as rough and tough as the boys. We had to be if we wanted to play any games with them.'

'What were the games?'

'Can't you imagine?' Cindy laughed. 'Football mostly, or baseball.'

'And who won?'

'Neither. We usually ended up having fist fights until the teacher came along and managed to break us up and for doing so he was promptly rewarded with a letter-box filled with eels we'd caught in a stream not far from the school.'

'Glad you made the break and came to Auckland?'

'Yes, I am. I went to boarding school in Wellington, but I didn't care for the city very much and the only other city was Palmerston North, but that was too close to home, so it had to be Auckland. I've always wanted to visit Auckland.'

'And what about a boy-friend? You must have a sweetheart back home to whom you've promised faithfully you would return? Someone who makes your heart turn a somersault every time you think of him?' Stuart's narrowed eyes were watching her, their brilliance not dulled at all by the smoke in the air.

He was laughing at her, Cindy realized. He seemed to know all about what made a woman tick, all her desires and emotions and even those which a woman likes to consider secret. All in all, he knew just too much about women. 'How would you know about the emotions of anyone's heart when you don't even have one yourself!' Cindy snapped and wished immediately she hadn't. What a thing to say!

However, his attitude didn't alter. He merely leaned over and took her hand inside his coat and placed her palm against his shirt. Beneath her palm she felt his hardness and warmth and also the even thud of a beating heart. 'Convinced?' he murmured softly, his eyes not leaving hers.

Trying hard to hide the calamity of emotions scrambling through her at his contact, she drawled: 'Well, well, wonders never cease.' She withdrew her hand and glanced at her watch. 'Six-fifteen, Mr. Newman, some overtime.'

'But you enjoyed it, didn't you? And also we both found it educational.'

'In what way?' She should have known better than to ask.

'You discovered I had a heart while I discovered I like the feel of your hand over it. Don't you think that it's a start which could lead to bigger and better things?'

'For you perhaps, Mr. Newman, but not for me.' Cindy stood up quickly, leaving her coffee untouched. 'Thank you for the dinner, it was lovely, but if you'll excuse me, I must get my shopping done.'

'Not so fast.' Stuart also stood up and signalled to the waiter, paid him and then taking Cindy's arm he led her out of the restaurant.

'Now what do you want?' Cindy asked, exasperated.

'You forget I owe you for one badly stained dress.'

'You don't owe me anything.'

'Oh, but I do, and I insist on buying you another. And honey, try not to look so pleased about life in general,' he said and slid his fingers along the inside of her wrist, down until his hand was warmly clasped about her cold one. Immediately she tried to pull her hand free from the thrill of his caressing fingers, but was unsuccessful.

She looked away from him, so big and tall beside her. She was tall herself but only came up to his shoulder. She was aware of girls glancing in open admiration at Stuart as they passed by on the pavement and felt a sudden thrust of pride at their envy of her. Oh, what the heck, he was an attractive guy, charming and amusing, so, as long as it didn't go any further than a casual dinner date with him, why shouldn't she enjoy it?

'Come on, smile for me,' he said softly.

She turned back to him, to find his dark head bent close to hers. Conceited ape! She started to glare at him, but suddenly she broke down and laughed helplessly.

'That's the way!'

'You really are conceited, aren't you?'

'If you say so. Now let's make for the 246 and get you a dress.'

'Oh, not there. They're much too expensive, besides the one which was stained was only homemade and the stain has been drycleaned out.' Then taking a look at his set expression, one which was becoming all too familiar, she decided to save her breath.

The 246 was indeed an impressive store, catering for everything, but not so much for every pocket. Glass show cases displayed all sorts of merchandise arranged simply but effectively.

Inside, the store was bright and modern and spaciously set out and also oddly quiet, the carpets muffling the sound of footsteps.

They made their way up an escalator to the Mantle Department. Stepping off the escalator Stuart stopped when confronted by a sign on which was written: 'Lingerie Department'. Beyond this were displayed various items of women's underclothing and then the Mantle Department.

For the first time Cindy caught sight of an expression of obvious discomfort on Stuart's face and almost laughed aloud. Never yet had she ever been with a man who would venture into a department of a shop such as this. Even her father, when she and her mother made an infrequent visit to Palmerston North, would rather stand outside on the pavement and watch people walking back and forth rather than enter any shop with them. Now seeing this side of Stuart amazed her as well as it warmed her. He seemed more human somehow, experiencing such a thing as embarrassment and feeling somewhat ridiculous and out of place, and not so much the suave self-assured man of the world.

'What are we waiting for? The Mantle Department is just through here. See it?' Cindy urged impishly, looking away from him to where she was pointing so as not to let him see the corners of her lips twitching uncontrollably.

'Hang on a minute!' He grabbed her hand. 'Let's go around this way.'

'What for? This way is quicker . . .'

But he had pulled her away and walked her swiftly through the Toy Department into the Mantle Section. She could almost picture him wiping his forehead and running his fingers around the collar of his shirt — an action so absurdly out of character for him, that she began to laugh.

He looked down at her.

'Phew, that was a near escape, wasn't it?' she grinned.

'Why — you little witch! You knew, and yet you would have dragged me through all those half-dressed figures just for laughs!'

'I didn't know you held such strong objection to half-dressed women,' she mocked.

'Ah — half-dressed women, but half-dressed plastic figures — there is a difference you know!'

'Oh, of course,' Cindy nodded. 'I'll take your word for it.'

'One soft and warm — the other hard and cold. Which category do you come under, Cindy Taylor?'

Cindy looked away from him and, dragging him by the hand, she said flippantly: 'That, Stuart Newman, is none of your business.'

He laughed and, allowing himself to be sidetracked,

he followed her lead towards the racks of brightly coloured frocks.

'Oh, I don't know,' Cindy groaned after pulling out one dress after another and then putting them back.

Finally, a woman assistant who had managed to get away from one demanding customer, approached them, smiling. 'Can I help you?'

Stuart turned and bestowed upon the woman one of his most charming lopsided smiles, which wouldn't fail to turn even the coldest female heart. Cindy grinned to herself at his overflow of charm for the assistant and felt a thrill course through her as he openly sought her hand and held it. 'Madam would like a wool dress, preferably olive green and something out of the ordinary.'

The assistant nearly bent over backwards to please them, showing them almost every frock she had in stock.

'I see I'm going to have to take you along on all my shopping expeditions if it means getting this kind of service,' Cindy whispered to Stuart.

At last, with about four which Stuart had chosen draped over her arm, the assistant led Cindy towards a dressing room and helped her into one. Zipping her up, the woman said: 'Leave it on and I'll bring your husband in and see what he thinks.'

Before her words had time to register, the woman had left. Cindy shrugged and turned this way and that in front of the full length mirror and stood waiting for Stuart's reaction as he entered the dressing room.

'Well, what do you think? You have chosen the right colour for your wife, it suits her beautifully,' the assistant remarked, standing with her hands folded in front of her. Immediately, Cindy glimpsed at the wicked gleam which came into his eyes. 'Don't you think so?'

Stuart ignored the obvious message Cindy was flashing him. Instead he grinned and let his eyes wander over her. Then after having taken his time, enjoying her discomfort and sensing her rising anger, he nodded: 'Beautiful,' he said.

'The style is nice but very plain. Perhaps her being so tall she would suit something more stylish.' The assistant was speaking exclusively to Stuart, as though she had forgotten Cindy was even present, much less the one who was going to purchase the dress and had to wear it.

Before she was aware of what was happening the assistant had turned her around and was unzipping the frock. Desperately, Cindy turned her head and stared at Stuart appealingly until the green material passed over her eyes. The assistant pulled the frock over her head, shook it free of its creases and hung it deftly back on its hanger and then began unzipping the next one.

Never before had she known herself to blush, but now, as Stuart's amused eyes took in every detail of her appearance as she stood in her brief white mini-slip, Cindy felt heat creep slowly up over her skin. She wasn't quite sure whether it was caused by embarrassment or anger. She glared at him through tangled brown hair which she brushed back viciously. She took the second dress from the woman, struggled into it, jerked up the zip and blew the remaining tangled strands of hair from her eyes.

'Mmm — not bad. What do you think — darling?'

'Ohhh!' she fumed. Silently she struggled in and out of the remaining two dresses and listened as Stuart and the assistant exchanged criticisms and opinions.

'I think the second one, don't you — darling? Would you like to try it on again?' Stuart said, his eyes sparkling wickedly.

'No, I'll take the second one. I like it too,' Cindy managed pleasantly. 'I'll kill him for this!' she vowed to herself. 'And that dumb woman, if she'd stop ogling at that creep she'd see that I don't wear a wedding ring.'

Finally, when she was dressed in her own clothes and had tidied up, she went to join Stuart who was waiting for the dress to be wrapped. '*You* — you're the absolute limit!' Cindy muttered vehemently. 'How dare you let her believe that — that we were married? *How dare you* take advantage of the situation which you deliberately evoked. Being so charming to her that she didn't even bother to see if I had a wedding ring on . . .'

'Hmmm, a very educational evening,' Stuart grinned, her anger bouncing off him without penetrating at all.

'And very one-sided!'

'At the moment — just for the present,' he was eager to assure her, 'I like it this way. I would say you came under the category of being very soft and very warm; you speak like a fishwife and also you have a tiny mole on . . .'

'*Stuart*, please!'

Stuart raised an eyebrow. 'Oh, it's Stuart now, eh? We're getting along famously. Improving all the time.'

'Oh, you don't care, do you? You would've carried on like that if I had been trying on a bikini. You're despicable, hateful and I hate you, hate you, hate you . . .'

'Now don't tell lies. You like me, so why bother to deny it? Besides, it wasn't as if you were trying on a bikini. You looked just as delectable in that slip thing you wore.'

Cindy cast him a withering glance and went stalking on ahead of him onto the downward escalator.

However, he was close behind her. 'Oh, come on, honey. I've seen more women that I can count who have had on much less than you. Anyway every woman likes to be told that she's desirable.'

'I'm not every woman, Mr. Newman!'

Stuart rolled his eyes heavenward and slapped his hand down on the moving rubber railing, making a loud cracking sound. 'So, back to Mr. Newman!'

Cindy remained silent.

'Where else do you have to go?'

'Just to get a scarf. I'll need it now that I've lost my rain hat.'

'Is that a dig at me?'

Cindy shrugged, and stopping at the Accessory Department she started looking through the array of scarves.

'Pale blue,' Stuart said.

'I like the cherry red.' Cindy picked up the bright chiffon scarf and paid for it, then thrust it, wrapped, into her handbag.

'Where to now?'

'I'm going home, and seeing I had to go to so much trouble to get it, I'll take the dress.' She almost snatched the parcel from him.

'Sure. It'll look better on you than it would on me,' he attempted to make her smile but failed. 'Let's get along then and I'll run you home.'

'No, thanks. I'll get a taxi.'

'Look, don't be so childish. What use is there in you getting a taxi when I can run you home in a few minutes?' He took her arm and refused to relinquish his hold until they reached his car. His expression was set and determined and his hold ruthless.

He unlocked the door of the car and helped her in. With a twist she was out of his hold and slammed the door. Suddenly her blood ran cold as she heard him give a groan of pain. Forcing herself to move, she climbed out of the other door as fast as she could without jerking the car too much and ran around to where Stuart, almost ashen with pain, had freed his hand.

'Oh, Stuart, I'm sorry — I'm sorry!' She fought back her panic and bent to inspect his hand.

'Well, it doesn't look as though I've lost it, but it damn well felt like it,' he laughed grimly, and gritted his teeth as she touched it.

'It's a bad gash, Stuart. It looks as though it might need stitches.' Cindy ran her tongue over her dry lips.

'Stitches, hell!' Stuart growled. 'Can you bandage?'

'Yes, but . . .'

'But nothing. The hotel is just here, I have a suite on the top floor — you can fix it up, that is if you're not too squeamish.'

'Of course I'm not! I've looked after wounded animals most of my life. There have been some worse wounds than this.'

Stuart merely grunted. He handed her a bunch of keys and with awkward movements, wrapped his handkerchief around his hand.

He led her through the hotel foyer to the lift and pushed the button for the top floor. He told her which key to use when they stopped outside the last door of the passage which was marked 'Private'.

Inside, the rooms were cool and smelled pleasantly of polish and cleanliness. Other than the fact that they were beautifully furnished with luxurious items of furniture and in colours of rich green and pale gold, Cindy didn't have the time nor inclination to notice anything else.

Stuart led the way to a large bathroom and pulled open the door to the cabinet above the wash-basin. 'Okay, there's the necessary equipment. Do your stuff!' He sat on the edge of the bath and she was uncomfortably aware of his close scrutiny, his watching every movement.

She bathed his hand and applied the appropriate dressing which surely must have hurt him, but he never flinched. With a swift upward glance she found his eyes still fixed on her and that his skin had turned slightly grey. She bandaged his hand as securely as she could. 'There, that will be okay for the time being, but I still think you should go to the hospital and see if it needs to be stitched.'

'That's fine. Thanks a lot.'

Bravely she looked up at him as he stood up. 'I'm sorry, Stuart. It was all my fault. If I hadn't have carried on so — so childishly this wouldn't have happened.'

Stuart smiled, and bringing up his good hand he brought the palm of it over her forehead and smoothed down her disordered hair on the top of her head, then tipped her chin up with a knuckle. 'Forget it, honey. It's all part of your growing up. It's natural for a girl to resent a man who lightheartedly treads all over things she values most.'

'But — but I'd rather it happened to me than to have you suffer the pain of it.'

He watched as her eyes filled with tears and felt amazed. 'Well, well,' he murmured softly and gently removed the tears clinging to her lashes, with his finger. 'This is the first time a woman has ever cried over me. You know that?'

Cindy shook her head. 'I'm sorry.'

'I'm not. It's rather pleasant for a change. Now forget it and turn on that dazzling smile of yours. It's not the end of the world.' He put an arm around her and squeezed her shoulders, then left her.

Unthinkingly she followed him and stopped abruptly at the door of his bedroom. He was stripping off his blood-stained shirt and bare from waist up, he searched through a drawer and withdrew a black polo-neck pullover.

He laughed at her embarrassment. 'You really are a child, aren't you?'

'C-can you manage — with your hand?'

'I'll get you to help me on with my coat.' His eyes were laughing, but she was only too willing to do something for him. She held the coat and waited for him to shrug into it, before buttoning it up the front.

'Honey?'

'Yes?' She stared up at him.

'I hate to put you to so much trouble, but I don't wear my coat buttoned up,' he grinned.

Suddenly, Cindy was perilously near to tears again. 'Oh, I'm sorry.' Quickly she unbuttoned it.

'Come on, kid, I'll drive you home. You look all in.' He spoke with such gentleness that Cindy found herself raising her eyes to his.

CHAPTER FOUR

'I HAD A letter from Mum yesterday,' Jo said.

'Mmmm,' Cindy stood gazing out of the living-room window at the bleak grey clouds hanging low over the Bay turning the usual vivid blue waters a grey-green colour. She listened absently to the clicking of Jo's needles as she sat busily knitting a set of tiny baby's garments and this, being her first attempt at knitting anything quite so tricky, she was doing very well.

'Cindy,' Jo prodded.

'Oh, I'm sorry, Jo. I was miles away. What were you saying?' With an effort, Cindy turned her attention away from the view and pushed all other thoughts from her mind.

'I said I had a letter from Mum yesterday. She wants us all to go down for next week-end. Would you like to go?'

'Yes, I'd love to. It's been ages since I've seen your Mum and Dad.'

Jo sighed. 'You still seem miles away. Won't you tell me what's bothering you? You've been pretty quiet all week. There is nothing wrong, is there?'

Cindy shook her head and turned back to the window. Jo put down her knitting and went to stand by her cousin. 'Come on, Cindy, spill it. I know there's something on your mind.' She put an arm around her shoulders and gave them a gentle shake.

'I just wish I didn't know, that's all.'

'Didn't know what?'

'It was you, wasn't it — you and Stuart?'

Immediately Jo let her arm fall, an expression of pain flickered across her face for a second and then blankness replaced it. She went back to her chair and took up her knitting.

'So Stuart told you, did he?' she sighed resignedly.

'No! I mean yes — but not on purpose, Jo. He thought I already knew. Oh Jo, I'm sorry, I didn't really want to know anything about it. It's none of my business. I didn't know whether I should tell you I knew or not.'

'How long have you known?'

'Almost a week. That night it was raining. I didn't get a taxi, instead Stuart ran me home.'

'What exactly did he tell you?'

'Not much. Just that you were once in love with him, or thought you were. He was cruel about it. It didn't seem to worry him that he may have hurt you. He told me about the baby too.'

'What about it?'

'Well, that you more or less had to get married.'

'The baby is Keith's, Cindy.'

Cindy turned back to the window and closed her eyes thankfully.

'Did Stuart say it wasn't?' Jo demanded.

'No — no, he didn't really tell me much at all. Just enough to leave behind niggling doubts.' Suddenly, Cindy turned to face her cousin. 'Jo, you are happy, aren't you — I mean really happy?'

'Of course I'm happy. I have every reason to be, haven't I? A husband, a baby coming, a new home and all the luxuries to go with it.'

'No, that's not what I meant. I mean, you are in love with Keith, aren't you, not Stuart still?'

'Stuart's past, but he's a person once known never forgotten. What I felt for him and what I now feel for Keith are entirely different. I'm glad I married Keith and if I had the opportunity over again I'd still marry Keith.'

'I'm glad. I was terribly afraid that you were unhappy.'

'I would have been far unhappier if I had married

72

Stuart. You see Stuart never did love me and I knew that. He never made any pretence that he did.

'I was young and foolish when I first came to Auckland. I was ready to be swept off my feet by the first guy who came along and there were quite a few before Stuart. When I met Stuart though, it was different. I did fall in love. He was every girl's dream and I think just about every girl who went out with him felt the same way and gave into him knowing that he didn't and never would love. I lasted longer than his previous girl-friends. That was until Delia came along,' Jo paused and then gave a mirthless laugh. 'Beautiful Delia. It was she who managed to take his disillusioned but vulnerable heart from hiding and then smashed it when she had it firmly within her grasp. She took off and married some Aussie business tycoon who was staying at the Southern Cross Hotel. I don't know what the reason was or why she did it.

'Then after Delia threw him over he came to me. I caught him on the rebound, but I was satisfied, for I thought that now there might be hope for me, but no. Stuart vowed that he would never let another woman make a fool of him. I could've killed Delia at the time and probably would have too, if she hadn't been in Aussie.'

There was silence except for the slow clicking of Jo's needles. 'You do see why I didn't want you to have anything to do with him, don't you? He was hard and cruel when I knew him first, he'll be even worse now. He was always hard and cynical, disillusioned with life and women right from the beginning, especially women. I don't know what made him refuse to accept women as anything but chattels made for the pleasure of man. He never at any time let on or told me about his past.'

'Poor Stuart . . .' Cindy murmured.

'Poor Stuart!' Jo hooted sarcastically. 'Poor Stuart nothing. There's absolutely nothing poor about Stuart Newman, there never was and never will be. He can take care of himself. Just how do you think he's got where he is today at his age if he couldn't? Riding roughshod over everybody, breaking them, using them and throwing them over when it suited him and he'll do the same with you. You're something new and different to him and holds attraction for him like a toy does for a child, and like a child he'll smash it when he's tired of it, and believe me that's very quickly. A spoilt child always tires of his things quickly.'

Jo went on after a while: 'I couldn't bear to see what happened to me also happen to you. Even in my home-town I was looked down upon, for my actions soon got around and it wasn't long before my name was mud.' Jo watched Cindy's face and then sighed. 'Ah, I know what you're thinking. You're thinking: "But with me it'll be different." Haven't I just told you — don't you think every girl thinks that? But it never is.'

Cindy shook her head.

'For your own sake I hope that's not what you're thinking,' Jo told her. 'Tread lightly, where he's concerned.'

The following week drifted along peacefully enough, with a great deal of talk about a forthcoming party which the staff were giving on Saturday night for the hotel's Head Chef who was leaving to go overseas, to bigger and much more worthwhile game in Australia.

'Are you going to this party that's being put on for Lucas?' Stuart asked as Cindy placed Friday's letters on his desk for his signature.

'No, I don't think so.'

'Why not? If it's a matter of transport I can pick you up and run you home without any bother,' Stuart offered.

74

'No, it's not that. Keith wouldn't mind bringing me in.'

'Oh, I see, no partner eh? Well, just this once I'll break the rules and escort you myself, then that'll be two problems done away with.'

Cindy looked at him, exasperated. 'How overwhelmingly generous of you,' she said scathingly. 'I sincerely hope that I'm not considered so unattractive that it's immediately taken for granted that I won't have a partner.'

'Well, have you? No, and nor have I, so why haggle over trivial vanities? I'll pick you up at eight and make sure you're ready on time, I don't like hanging around.'

'No, of course not. It might prove a little awkward, not to mention embarrassing for you,' Cindy muttered ambiguously.

Stuart shot her a look which told her that he was well aware of what she was getting at. Saying no more he collected together the sealed letters and left the office.

With a slight shrug, Cindy re-entered her own office and after leaving it reasonably tidy, she slipped on her coat and made her way towards the foyer where she stopped abruptly.

Stuart was standing at the entrance talking to a woman and by the look on the woman's face and the way Stuart was holding her arm, Cindy guessed that theirs wasn't just a casual acquaintance. She watched as Stuart put his hand against her back and lead her outside towards the hotel staff's car park.

'So he didn't have a partner to take along to this farewell party, eh?' Cindy thought, her eyes darkening in sudden anger. 'What made him ask me when he could have taken her? Was he feeling sorry for me? Surely not, he's not the type, but then I'm not his type, not like her.' A sensation like she had never known before gripped her, leaving her powerless to do anything but clasp and unclasp her hands. Jealousy. She was jealous of that unknown woman. 'Jo was right. He's not for any girl — and especially not for me. He's as unattainable as the moon and his heart even more so, but I wish I didn't mind so much.'

It wasn't until she was almost home that she suddenly realized that the real reason for not attending the party was because she was going with Jo and Keith to Putaruru to spend the week-end with Jo's parents. 'Good grief, now what am I going to do?'

'Ring him up and tell him that you can't possibly go with him!' Jo announced angrily, while Cindy was helping her set the table for dinner. 'What on earth made you say you'd go with him in the first place?'

'I don't know. I didn't even say I'd go. Before I knew where I was he had arranged everything and was gone.'

'How typical! Well, just get on that phone now and tell him that you won't be going!'

Reluctantly, Cindy searched through the directory for his number. Dialling it, she called to Jo, remembering the woman she had seen him with: 'He probably won't be home.'

'He'd better be!'

Cindy quickly turned her attention to the phone as she heard someone answering. A woman's voice greeted her and stated the number. Cindy froze as though she had been paralysed. For the life of her she couldn't speak.

'Hello. Are you there?' the voice repeated and then faintly Cindy heard her say: 'No one's answering, darling. Must be someone fooling around . . .' followed by a click as the receiver was slammed back down onto its cradle.

Feeling sick with misery and jealousy, Cindy slowly hung up and went back out to the kitchen.

She shook her head at Jo's inquiring glance. 'No answer.'

'You look pale, honey. Look, I'm sorry I snapped at you the way I did. Don't take it too much to heart. Ring up later on tonight and if there is still no answer then it can't be helped. There'll be other week-ends to visit Mum and Dad.'

'What can I say? I'm really sorry, Jo.'

'Forget it. Stuart has that kind of effect on women.' She spoke jokingly but there was still a slight frown puckering her brow.

Later that night, Cindy rang Stuart once more and even more reluctantly, her stomach tying itself up in knots caused by fear and nerves, dreading what she might hear. However, this time there was no answer and with something almost like relief, she hung up.

'Still no reply?' Jo asked as Cindy re-entered the living-room.

She shook her head. 'No, I'm afraid not.' And upon hearing Jo's sigh of exasperation she added: 'But you and Keith must still go tomorrow. Your parents will be terribly disappointed if you don't.

'It's you they'll be disappointed in not seeing. I'll tell you what. Instead of going for the week-end, we'll leave early on Sunday morning and go for the day. I don't fancy leaving you here by yourself and especially not in the clutches of a wolf like Stuart.'

'Oh Jo,' Cindy laughed. 'Don't worry about me. I have no intention of falling under his spell. We're no longer together for five minutes and we're at each other's throats. Now don't argue. It's my fault all this has happened. All that air up in the high country will do you good and I know you'd like to see your family again, so you're not going to be done out of it just because of me.'

The next morning at eight-thirty, Cindy waved good-bye to Jo and Keith and went back into the house to clear away the soiled breakfast dishes and tidy up.

There had been a white frost earlier that morning but the sun was fast melting it and drying the wet dew, a sure promise of a beautiful warm day ahead.

To fill in her time, Cindy decided to go for a swim early that afternoon and so dressing warmly in slacks and jumper, she strolled down to the Bay and changed into her bathing suit in the bathing sheds on the parade.

There were a few people swimming, none of whom stayed in for very long. The water was clear and cold, but deliciously so, splashing over her causing her to gasp and splutter.

There was no sign of the sea where she came from for the little town of Apiti was situated at the foot of the Ruahine Range, one of three mountain Ranges running up the centre of the lower part of the North Island, where in the winter snow covered most of the ground but soon thawed when sunny weather prevailed.

Dripping and shivering slightly, Cindy climbed up onto the pale sandy beach. She rubbed herself vigorously with a rough towel and then lay back and closed her eyes, feeling the welcome rays of the sun on her skin. The only discomfort that told her it was winter was the cool breeze coming up over the sea's calm surface.

Throughout that day she managed to keep all thought of Stuart from her mind, but when the time came for her to get ready for the party, she could feel the excitement mounting within her. She couldn't quell it no matter how she tried and through this she managed to ladder one pair of nylons, catch the heel of her shoe in the hem of her dress and ruin her make-up so that she had to remove it and try again.

By the time eight o'clock came she was in a fearful temper, conducting hate sessions with herself and perilously near to tears of temper. She quickly composed herself when she heard the door bell ring and after taking a swift glance at her appearance in the full length mirror she went down the hall to answer the door, feeling the heavy crêpe folds of her dress swirl around her.

She opened the door to Stuart and in the semi-darkness of the porch all she could see was the large frame of his body and the white of his shirt.

'Come in,' she greeted him shortly. 'I'll just fetch my coat. I won't be a minute.' She left him in the hall while she went to gather her handbag and gloves from the top of her bed and slip her bluish-grey coat from its hanger.

As she approached him in the hall she felt her pulses warm her body as his appreciative gaze roved over her.

She knew she looked lovely in the flowing white crêpe dress she wore. Gathered softly at the neck, it fell in heavy folds to just above the knee. It was styled to leave her shoulders and arms completely bare and the neck was caught by a high stand-up collar covered with silver sequins to match the silver lurex glittering elusively in the white material.

'I was going to say you look very lovely, but I don't like to risk getting my head snapped off,' he drawled.

'What do you mean?' Cindy asked as he held the coat for her to slip into.

'Well, I didn't get what you'd call an overwhelming welcome, did I?'

Cindy laughed apologetically. 'I'm sorry, but everything just seemed to be going wrong.'

'Last minute nerves?'

'You flatter yourself!' Cindy flashed. 'It just so happen's that I'm a bit put out because I should have been going away with Jo and Keith this week-end.'

'Blow it!' she said to herself. She hadn't meant to reveal this to him, for with his razor sharp mind he would probably find something in it which would be to his advantage and would flatter his ego, but what he did come up with put her completely off balance.

After he had helped her into his car, he slipped in beside her and switched on the ignition. 'So it was you who rang up last night.'

'Last night?' Cindy echoed, a cold sense of dread creeping through her.

'Come on, baby, don't act so damn innocent. Why didn't you answer Marty? Don't tell me you were paralysed with shock or jealousy?'

Cindy caught her breath at the truth in his added remark.

'I suppose you rang later too, hmmm?' He laughed softly when she didn't reply.

'Oh, stop laughing, for heaven's sake!' Cindy snapped furiously. 'I suppose you think it's hilarious to have all these women running after you. Well, that doesn't worry me if they're so stupid, but if you're expecting me to be the same as the rest of them then you can go jump off the top of Mount Eden. It seems that you should have taken Marty, or whatever her name is, to this do tonight doesn't it, because I have no intention of paying for tonight's entertainment, if that's what one can call it?' Even to her own ears she sounded crude and she could have howled. Here they were, together for not more than five minutes, and fighting already.

'Honey, Marty is a woman, you're nothing but a baby. What on earth gave you the idea that I would want "payment", as you so delicately described it, from you?'

Cindy flinched, recognizing his insulting way of putting her in her place. 'You don't fool me. I'm not that much of a baby. You'd take what you could get if it was offering. Try to deny it.'

He laughed. 'Okay, I won't deny it. Why should I?

I might be ruining my own chances where you're concerned.'

Cindy could do nothing, for a moment, but gape at him through the dim interior of the car. 'You're just unbeatable — you know that? There wouldn't be another insufferable boor quite like you in the whole of this world.'

'Spare me the descriptions of my disreputable character. We'll discuss it when we find out which one of us is right.'

She turned away from him, her lips clamped tightly together and her anger trying vainly to win against the trembling of her hands and the awareness of that same dangerous excitement which he had managed to create in her the first time they had met.

'Have Jo and Keith gone away for the week-end regardless of tonight's engagement?'

'Yes!'

'I'm surprised,' he said meaningfully.

'You needn't be. Jo was against my going with you, however, I assured her that she didn't have the slightest need to worry.'

'Even in spite of the fact she knew that you would rather go out with me than with her and Keith?'

'I would not! . . . Just what do you mean?'

'Or didn't she know of the outcome of your phone call? Did you tell her that I was out? That's evidence enough, isn't it?'

'Why do you always have to go all out to prove to yourself that every girl is susceptible to you — every girl without exception?'

'Is that what it appears like to you? Well, that wasn't my intention. You're the one who is so adamant about not being susceptible that I'm going all out to prove to *you* that you're wrong. I've got a prize at stake.'

Cindy didn't wonder so much at his last remark, but the tone in which he spoke it. 'You think all women are tarred with the same brush just because you've been let down by a few . . .'

'So far I've been proven right and I have no belief that just because you're younger you're different.' Stuart brought the car to a halt, parking it outside the Southern Cross Hotel.

'Then I'm sorry you think that way.'

'Being sorry can't alter the fact that I have yet to be proven wrong,' he spoke harshly and jerking open the door, he got out and came around to open the door for her.

Glancing down at his hand, across which was applied a wide strip of plaster, she asked: 'How is your hand now?'

He looked down at it. 'Oh that, a mere scratch. It's healing fine.' He flashed her a sudden grin and immediately warmth eased through her chilled body.

She smiled back. 'This is a much better feeling than when we fight,' she thought, and confidently, happily, she gave a tiny skip beside him and allowed his hand to unglove hers. He put the glove in his pocket and entwined his fingers with her cold ones.

He didn't let her hand go even after they had entered the hotel and were approaching the section which was often let for private parties, functions and business purposes.

'Do you think we should hold hands like this, here in the hotel?' she whispered worriedly.

He smiled, his pulse-quickening, lopsided smile. 'Are you forgetting? Tonight we're breaking the rules, so why shouldn't we go the whole hog?'

He felt her slim fingers tighten a fraction on his and he gave a tiny smile of satisfaction. 'A little longer and bit of luck, despite all her virtuous ideas, she's the same as the rest of them.' He thought of the stag head.

After leaving her coat in the Powder Room, Cindy returned to Stuart's side, and followed him as he led the way towards a table where a man and girl were sitting, both of whom Cindy was sure she hadn't seen at the hotel before, but somehow the man's face seemed familiar. Stuart appeared to know him too, for they greeted each other by shaking hands.

The man then turned to Cindy, his bold eyes frankly admiring, but Cindy didn't mind, for he looked open faced and good fun. She smiled at him and sat down on the chair Stuart pulled out for her. 'And who is this?' he asked Stuart, his eyes not leaving her face.

'My secretary, Cindy Taylor.'

'You're a bright one. I thought you made certain rules in this hotel of yours.'

Stuart shrugged. 'In some cases rules are made for breaking.'

'But not certain promises, eh?'

Stuart ignored this and introduced his friend as Paul Brent and the girl with him was introduced as Sharon Palmer.

Feeling acutely uncomfortable at the interest Paul Brent was showing in her, Cindy glanced at Sharon to see if she was resenting this at all, but to her amazement Sharon seemed to have forgotten all about Paul as her eyes, beneath their heavy make-up and false eyelashes, were focused firmly on Stuart. In turn, she looked around at Stuart and with a shiver of delight, she found that his eyes had been exploring the nape of her neck and the way in which she had pinned her hair up into a smooth pleat.

As her glance locked with his, she heard him whisper: 'You're very lovely.' While this remark and the way in which he said it, together with the look he gave her, made her thrill with excitement, she thought sadly, her throat tightening: 'It comes so easy to him. Whether he means it or not, he's still out to prove himself right.' She gave him a small smile, but before she turned away he glimpsed at the momentary flicker of sadness in her expression and felt vaguely irritated.

'Would you care to dance?' Paul asked her, almost to a point of rudeness in excluding his partner.

Hesitating, Cindy thought: 'If I dance with him, Stuart will probably dance with Sharon.' But seeing that there was not much else she could do, she smiled and stood up.

Paul was not unlike Stuart in physique, but there the resemblance ended. Paul could be considered much better looking, for his features were more regular and his colouring was definitely fair, dark blond hair and blue eyes.

His personality was gay and carefree and boldly charming. As he danced he made an attempt to hold her closer, but rigidly she held herself away and heard him laugh and say softly: 'You suit that dress, ice-maiden. Is Stuart in for the cold treatment too?'

At his mention of Stuart, Cindy darted a look at their table and brightened considerably as she found that he wasn't dancing with Sharon after all. Instead, he was sitting listening to what she was saying but with his eyes following every movement that she and Paul were making.

When the dance had ended, Paul took her back to their table and with a wink at her, said to Stuart: 'Like dancing with an ice-box, but she assures me that she'll defrost a little for you.'

'I said no such thing!' Cindy gasped, embarrassed by Stuart's laughing gaze upon her.

'Shall we find out, eh?' He pressed the butt of his cigarette into an ashtray and taking her hand he led her out onto the floor.

From the corner of her eye she saw Sharon's disappointed, sulky expression, but soon forgot her as she danced with Stuart, his arm firmly about her and his hand hard against her back.

He was a good dancer but because of the overcrowded floor and the younger members of the staff, who not knowing how to dance, resorted to half twisting and jiving and half waltzing, there was little room to dance properly without getting clouted by someone's elbow and trodden on by kicking feet.

Cindy danced with Stuart for most of the evening. As the floor became more and more crowded, Stuart held her closer to him and although her instincts warned her to resist, she willingly moved closer. He bent his head to the side of hers and because he couldn't see her, she closed her eyes, letting herself drown in this fleeting moment of madness.

Suddenly she stiffened in his arms and her eyes flew open as she felt him bend his head and his lips brush the bare skin of her shoulder.

Quickly she moved back from him. The whole situation was dangerous and because she liked it so much she realized that it could swerve out of control if she didn't put a stop to him rousing these emotions within her.

When the last strands of music died away, Stuart asked: 'Would you like a drink?'

Cindy pressed her hands to her cheeks in an attempt to cool them. She shook her head. 'No, thanks. Gosh, isn't it hot in here?'

'We'll leave shortly after supper. Lucas' last in this hotel so we can't hurt his feelings by leaving and not having any,' Stuart grinned.

Impulsively, Cindy said: 'No — don't tell me — is that your heart speaking, or your stomach?'

'For a young thing you're criminally sarcastic.'

'I'm learning. I'm learning,' she said meaningly.

'Then you'd better quit, it doesn't suit you. Sarcasm is for the hard of this world and you're touchingly soft.' He seemed to be withdrawn from his earlier carefree mood, and for causing this withdrawal Cindy could have cried.

Stuart dutifully saw to it that she had enough to

eat and after the speeches, one upon which he was called to give, and saying good-bye to Paul and Sharon, they left.

Cindy breathed in deeply the cool night air as they went over to Stuart's car. She stared absently out of the window while Stuart drove through the busy streets, usual for late Saturday night.

'But this isn't the way to Mission Bay,' she spoke suddenly, sitting up, her drowsiness leaving her.

'I know. You haven't been up to the top of Mount Eden, have you?'

'No.'

'Well, seeing that you told me that I'd have to jump off rather than allow yourself to be conquered then I'll show you what kind of death you've prescribed for me.'

'What for?'

'Perhaps that soft heart of yours might take pity on me,' he laughed.

'If I did that then I'd have a soft head, not a soft heart,' she said dryly.

The powerful car twisted and turned its way to the top of the extinct volcano, the highest of many upon which the city of Auckland was built.

'Ohhh — it's breathtaking!' Cindy exclaimed.

'What is — my way to go?' Stuart leaned back against the door, looking at her.

'Oh, you!' Cindy turned on him with a mocked withering glance and opening the door she leapt out. Immediately the wind caught at her and with a struggle she managed to walk over towards the ridge of earth rising from the otherwise flat plateau.

Stuart sat watching her as the wind blew the yards of white-silver material against her and lifting the pins from her hair causing it to blow out across her face. He smiled as she turned and lifted out her arms to him. 'Come on. It's glorious, and the view — it's unbelievable!'

Suddenly the smile was wiped from his face as he saw her turn and start to walk on. His heart seemed to plunge painfully in fright. Shoving open the door he was out of the car and running towards her as fast as the wind would permit him. 'Cindy!' he shouted, but the wind carried his voice out behind him.

Whether it was a kind turn of fate or a strong thrust of determination on his part which gave him the extra speed to reach her side, he didn't know. All he was aware of was his blazing anger, so great that he wanted to shake her senseless. Angry at the fright she gave him and angry with himself for not having had the sense to warn her.

Grasping her bare upper arm, he wheeled her around to face him. Despite the unexpectedness of his action, her expression of wonder at the beauty spread below her, didn't alter. 'Isn't it utterly beautiful? Out of this world?' she said, dreamily, gesturing towards the sea of lights sprawling for miles below them. The Harbour Bridge, lit up, was reflected in the calmness of the Waitemata Harbour as were other city lights from the buildings situated along the curving edge of the Harbour. 'Like a fairyland, and up here, in our castle, we're the king and queen.'

'You stupid little fool!' he shouted at her, taking out his self-anger on her. 'One step further and you would have gone over the edge!'

Blinking, Cindy looked down to where he was pointing and sure enough there was a sheer drop below the side of the mountain, into a bottomless pit of darkness. 'Do very many people really commit suicide up here?' she asked blankly. Her voice still contained a rather far-away quality.

With his hands biting into the flesh of her arms, he pulled her to him and then bending his head, he kissed her hard on the mouth. At first his attack, unexpected as it was, caught her completely unawares so that all she was capable of doing was to remain passive and her body unyielding, while wild joy flared through her until she felt as though she would have buckled at the knees had Stuart not been holding her. But when he pulled her closer until his hold became painful and his mouth so hard that her own lips were numb, she panicked and began struggling. Frantically she put her hands up and tried to push his face away.

Finally, her fear got through to him and abruptly he let her go. His eyes looked down at her trembling figure, the rapid rise and fall of her breast caused by her breathless sobbing. Her eyes wide with shock in her pale face, stared up at him.

'You've — you've spoiled it. You've spoiled everything,' she said at last, in a choked whisper. She turned away from him, back towards the car, one hand going up to keep her hair from covering her face and the other holding her frock down against the wind.

'What have I spoiled? Your little girl illusions that up here is like being in a fairyland and that you and I are king and queen?' He caught up with her and flung her around to face him. He saw her flinch at the mimicking tone in his voice.

'It — it was lovely up here, not like being on earth at all. Now you spoiled what attraction it held for me. Now I hate it. Do you hear? I hate it up here!'

'Listen to me, you pious little so-and-so!' He grasped her shoulders and shook her. 'So you hate it up here? Lesson one: I can't help whether you hate it or not. There's nothing I can do that will turn the clock back and make you love it again. It's something you'll just have to take. You understand? Like you'll have to take a good many other knockbacks life has to offer. That's life and that's living.'

'Life and living means giving. Have you ever in

your life given instead of just taken?' Cindy said tightly.

His mouth tightened and his eyes, hard and cold, mocked her. 'Well, well, Cindy Taylor, a puritan, philosopher and some damn human angel of God all rolled into one!'

She shivered, suddenly feeling young and frightened and well out of her depth. Her eyes locked with his and her skin burned as his hands closed over her wrists, his fingers caressing the inside of her wrists. 'Baby, what do you know about life? Born and brought up in some one-horse town, sheltered and safe. You finally broke away and now find yourself in a big city where the pace of life is different and in the majority of cases, people are different too. You can't remain a country mouse here, Cindy my angel.' His voice was no longer sneering but low and seductive. 'You haven't lived yet but I could show you how to live. Together we could reach the very heights life has to offer and I promise you won't be disappointed.' His hands had left her wrists and were now moving along her arms.

He made no move to kiss her or even draw her closer. He was so sure of the effect his touch was having without doing either, despite what had happened a moment ago. Too sure of her and too sure of every girl.

Disturbed and angry, Cindy slapped his hands away from her. 'Don't touch me! I loathe you touching me!' she spat. 'I loathe you for what you've done to Jo and for what you're trying to do to me and just for kicks. Does your whole purpose in life revolve around playing around without responsibility? Well, if you call that reaching the heights of living then I want no part of it. It holds no attraction for me and certainly not with you! You disgust me and so do your ideas and outlooks.'

'And you disgust me. At least I know what my faults are. But since you have thought it necessary to inform me of them, let me inform you of a few of yours. You're nothing but a smug, preaching little hypocrite, clinging to your virtue for dear life in some vain hope that you'll find some placid, unimaginative, but safe and equally smug male who will be willing to utter all the appropriate words which, when all put together, spell marriage. I wouldn't become involved with you for the simple reason that, like leeches once your type dig their possessive tenacious claws in, it's hard to shake them off.'

Cindy had gone completely white. She stood with her hands clenched at her sides, staring at him. 'How I hate you!' she whispered.

'Oh, I don't mean it!' she cried after his retreating figure, but the wind carried her voice away leaving her shaking with cold and fear. For a fleeting moment there, before he had turned away, she thought she saw a flicker of loneliness in his face.

She climbed into the car and they sat in tense silence while Stuart drove her home. He pulled up alongside the kerb, got out and walked her up to the door. Taking the key from her hand he unlocked the door, handed her the key and waited for her to go inside.

Twisting the key around with shaky fingers, she stood looking down at it, not wanting to part with such ill feeling between them. 'I'm sorry I said what I did. I don't hate you.' She looked up at him earnestly, as though willing him to accept her apology.

'Why should you apologize? I deserved it. Don't be so damn self-sacrificial. It's irritating. I know that I'm not a very likeable guy,' he scowled.

'But you are. If you'd let yourself . . .'

He sighed tolerantly. 'I wish you'd stop seeing qualities into people that aren't, and never will be there. I'm a no good and I know it. Just accept me as I am and you'll be better off. Good night!' Shoving his hands into his trouser pockets, he turned to walk down the steps and down the path to his car.

CHAPTER FIVE

ON MONDAY morning Cindy carried out her usual duties feeling tension mounting as she worked, half expecting Stuart to summon her into his office to give her notice. But all throughout that day and Tuesday, he never said a word about Saturday night.

First thing Wednesday, however, he did summon her, sounding unusually irate. 'Did you hear the news this morning?' he asked when she had entered his office.

Puzzled, she shook her head.

'Then take a look at this.' He threw a newspaper, one of many and all the same, on to his desk in front of her. She glanced at the headlines glaring at her in bold black print:

'In Palmerston North Last Night, Fire Destroyed Four Out of Six Motel Units'.

'Yours?' Cindy looked up.

'Of course they're mine!' Stuart snapped irritably. 'I'll have to travel down there and get started right away. I want you to book reservations for two at the Pioneer Hotel for at least two nights at bed and breakfast rate. And ask for concession. After you've done that, cancel any appointments I may have had for today, let the receptionist know we'll be away until Monday at least. I'll notify Bob and his wife. Bring your shorthand pad and pencil and I'll run you home to pack.' He was half way out the door when he turned back. 'I'll meet you in the car park in a half an hour. And don't, for God's sake, forget the mail!'

Dazed, Cindy remained motionless while his words sank through to her. 'Well, he said there would be travel included in my job but I had no idea I'd be given such short notice.'

In approximately twenty-five minutes, she had completed her tasks and was waiting down in the car park for Stuart. She saw him striding towards her, bareheaded and his overcoat flying open in the wind.

'Got the mail?'

She nodded.

'Good. I hope you can write in the car?'

Cindy felt her stomach heave slightly at this, thinking how sick she had been on the trip from Palmerston North to Auckland over the roads through the mountainous King Country. And having to travel with her head down, trying to write. 'Ugh!' she shivered.

'Well?' he prodded.

'Yes — yes, of course.'

'Fine. I hope Jo won't prove to be difficult by putting up objections.'

'Why should she? She trusts me.'

'Yeah, but I'm darn sure she doesn't trust me.'

'I think her trust of me would gain priority in this case,' Cindy retorted.

'Now don't start getting bitchy with me at this stage. Believe me I'm not in the mood to take it. I'll more than likely dump you in the middle of the Desert Road.'

'You'll probably have to dump me there anyway,' Cindy thought wryly. However, she was inwardly relieved at discovering that they were to take the roundabout route via the Desert Road which was longer but straighter and would cut the time of travel enormously.

It was obvious that Stuart had made this trip many times before for his powerful car ate up the miles at an alarmingly fast rate, while Cindy opened and read out the mail and took down Stuart's dictation which was slow in order that it would be easier for her.

However, they soon ran into a long stretch of windy road with the country towering on either side of them. It mostly consisted of green native bush rather than farming lands and it wasn't long before Cindy began to feel squirmy.

She closed her eyes for a moment trying to fight back the ghastly feeling rising from her stomach, but in the end, white-faced and feeling more and more like death, she looked up from her pad. 'Please — please stop!'

Stuart darted a swift glance at her and immediately brought the car to a halt at the side of the road.

She was out of the car like a shot and crossed quickly but unsteadily over the fence at the edge of the road and leaned over it. The fresh chilly wind blew welcomingly against her and she shut her eyes and lifted her face to it, smelling the fresh sweet odour of the bush.

'Are you okay?' Stuart strode over to her with her coat and attempted to put it around her shoulders, but weakly she protested. 'No — no, I don't want to be warm I feel much better already.' She added belatedly: 'I'm sorry to be such a nuisance.'

'You should've told me you got car-sick,' Stuart told her. 'Where that particular aspect was concerned, my previous secretary had the advantage of you.'

'Then you'd better decide which qualifications you like best! I can't help being car-sick. The roads are so windy!'

Stuart laughed shortly. 'I'm sorry for being so snarkey. This road won't last long. You can hang your head out of the window until we get on to a straighter stretch. The view will keep your mind off your tendency to be sick.'

He was right. It was only three hundred and forty-six miles from Auckland to Palmerston North, but within that distance they sped in and out of tiny and very lovely towns, many of which had Maori names that Cindy could sometimes correct Stuart in their romantic pronunciation. They travelled through the lush green, hilly country of the mighty Waikato, the pine forests and native bush of the great timber country, passed the Wairakei Stream Bores and around the shore line of Lake Taupo.

Around each bend or over each hill, it was as though a view had been specially placed in a position to greet them; always the mountainous hills, the trees and valleys, and perhaps a breathtaking view of the Waikato River or Lake Karapori far below them.

The Desert Road ran from Turangi to Waiouru. On each side of the road, New Zealand's desert country, usually so barren and wasted in the summer except for yellow-brown tussock grass, was now covered with glistening white snow. There were a few pines jutting up here and there, but other than these all attempts at putting the land to some profitable use up until now had failed.

Stuart drove carefully over the road's slippery, treacherous surface, while tirelessly, Cindy watched the sun on the white peaks and slopes of Mounts Ngauruhoe, Ruapehu and Tongariro so close beside them and in view all the way to Waiouru, while on the other side of the road, huge hills rose in the distance until the wide span of desert ended.

'I can't get over how beautiful it all is,' Cindy breathed. 'I've always wanted to travel overseas and people wonder why when we've got a part of every country in the world here at our feet — and a hundred times more beautiful. I can understand what they mean now. A paradise.'

Stuart laughed. 'Even when the roads are so windy that they make you sick?'

'The view compensates for that,' Cindy grinned. 'You've had a lucky escape. I could've taken the route over the Paraparas in the King Country. You would have known what it was to be car-sick then. The road is pretty good from now on though, except for some miles out of Taihape as we go over the Mangawekas, but if you concentrate on the view, you'll be okay.'

After about seven hours, with two stops, one at Taupo and one at Taihape, they approached the Manawatu District and for a change the country seemed flat. Even as they drove over Mount Stewart from where they could see the sprawling city of Palmerston North curved into the shape of a crescent some distance below them, the rise and descent was so gradual it was barely noticeable. However, the flatness contrasted greatly with the city's beautiful backdrop of three gigantic and lengthy Ranges, the Rimutakas, Tarruas and Ruahines, which half circled the Manawatu, dwarfing it as their higher peaks, some of which were covered with snow, pierced the blue sky.

They drove on towards the city. The impression created by the startling green of the country and wide blue skies simply oozed health, wealth and beauty.

'In what direction is Apiti from here?' Stuart asked as they sped along Rangitikei Line into Rangitikei Street which in turn led to the heart of the city.

'Over there, almost at the foot of the Ruahine Range.' Cindy waved her hand towards the Range of mountains and hills furthest away from the city.

'I thought so. Any snow yet, do you think?'

'I don't think so, but it won't be long by the feel of this wind.' Cindy hurriedly wound up the window to keep out the cold southerly winds Palmerston North was well known for.

'If we've got time on Friday how would you like me to run you over to see your parents? . . .'

The remainder of his sentence was left unfinished as Cindy exclaimed excitedly: 'Oh, would you? May I ring Mum and Dad tonight and let them know for sure? Maybe we could stay the week-end. They would be only too willing to put you up . . .'

'Hang on a minute! We'll have to see how things turn out over this blasted fire.' His smiling expression vanished as he became increasingly annoyed. 'We won't know exactly what's what until Friday, so we'll jack everything up then. Okay? And don't go building your hopes up. This may take longer than we think.'

The two days that followed were long and strenuous ones for Stuart and also for Cindy who accompanied him as he made several visits to his insurance company, assessors and solicitors, ready to take down various items and notes that he would later require.

Cindy could well understand Stuart's anger at his loss for the motel units completely ruined by fire had at one stage been profitable and popular too because of their situation. At the same time being close to the Square, the city's main shopping area, it was only a walk away from the bridge over the wide Manawatu River which had embanked along its sides a beautiful esplanade filled with blossom trees, native plants and shrubs, rose gardens and hothouses, picnic areas and lido swimming pool. All of which would attract the tourist who would naturally seek accommodation close by.

It was three on Friday afternoon before Stuart finally had all business matters settled and running smoothly and once more broached the subject of a possible trip to Apiti before leaving for Auckland.

'Well, now that we've done everything that can be done here, do you think we have time to make a quick trip to Apiti?' he said, lounging back in one of the vacant armchairs in the Hotel's lounge, stretching his arms above his head and looking at his watch.

97

'It's three-twenty. If we left for Auckland now we'd be there at about ten tonight, so it doesn't look like we'll have time.' He laid his head back and closed his eyes to the sun which was shining through the tall windows, onto his face.

'Oh, please, Stuart — I mean, Mr. Newman,' Cindy added hastily, seeing him open his eyes and regard her amusedly.

'Better leave it at Stuart. You've used it several times before now.'

'Oh, have I?' she said innocently.

'You know damn well you have.'

'Please can't we go? I can ring Mum and Dad now. They won't mind putting you up for the week-end, I've told you that.'

'Who said anything about the week-end? I may have a previous engagement tomorrow night.' His eyes closed.

Cindy blinked a little at this sudden enlightenment and then scowled, positive that he was fooling with her, 'Fink!' she thought. 'He's doing this on purpose.'

'Oh, well, if that's the case, then there's nothing else for it. Perhaps it's just as well in a way.'

'How's that?' he murmured with a pretence of drowsiness.

'I was just thinking — all that good fresh air and decent food may prove too great a shock to your system. You look puckered out now and this is just in Palmerston so goodness knows what you'll be like after a week-end in the Ranges, and also I doubt whether you'd be able to stand up to riding over those giant hills. You're not fit enough. It would take weeks before you'd recover. Maybe you can't even ride a horse . . .'

Stuart laughed. 'And you know — maybe you're right.' He leaned back and closed his eyes again, a silly grin on his face.

'Ohh!' Cindy stood up and gathering up her bag,

pad and pencil, she turned from him to go up to her room to pack.

'You'd better let your parents know that we're coming then. I wouldn't like to arrive late and miss out on any of that "decent food" you were telling me about,' Stuart called after her as she was just about to shut the door.

'Of all the stupid, exasperating . . .' Furious, Cindy slammed the door hard behind her, '. . . gorgeous hunks of men!' She laughed helplessly to herself and ran two steps at a time up the wide stairway to her room.

'Hi, Mum?' In her excitement she completely forgot to close the door to her room and looking up she saw Stuart lounging there looking half asleep, his hair ruffled and his eyes still half closed, watching her.

She gave him a grinning, exasperated look and then turned back, trying to concentrate on the dial face of the telephone, stabbing it constantly with her pencil. However, she was still aware of his large figure propped up against the door frame, casually dressed in a blue pullover and dark slacks and also aware, too, that she was sitting inelegantly on the bed with her legs crossed.

'Cindy?'

'Yes, Mum, it's me.'

'Where are you ringing from? I thought I heard the operator say this call was coming from Palmerston.'

'She did. I've been here for two days now.'

'Two days! What for? You're not in any trouble, are you?'

Cindy laughed. 'Do I sound as though I am? No, I travelled down here with Mr. Newman . . .'

'With whom?' Her mother interrupted.

'Mr. Newman, my boss.' Cindy could almost feel how closely Stuart was watching her and was beginning to get embarrassed. 'It must sound to him as though I never wrote and told Mum about my job,' she thought, annoyed. 'We're staying at the Pioneer Hotel, you know the new one that has just gone up on Pioneer Highway?'

'You've been staying with that man at the Pioneer Hotel for *two* days?'

Cindy felt herself turn hot and then cold at the tone of her mother's voice. 'Did she think that I was staying here with Stuart for — for . . . Surely not? But what did she mean by saying "that man" . . .'

'Mum! Of course not!' Cindy said aghast, completely forgetting Stuart's presence, to say nothing of his razor-sharp and perceptive mind.

He laughed and muttered behind his hand: 'Well, you did phrase that last sentence a little indelicately.'

Tossing her head, she turned away from him and spoke deliberately into the mouthpiece. 'Mr. Newman owns those motels that were burned down in Fitzherbert Avenue. He found he would need to come down here to see about different business matters in connection with the fires and he needed my assistance.' 'And just wait till I get home!' she thought to herself, hearing her mother's slightly relieved sigh.

'Mr. Newman said that if we had the time we could pop over and see you. We won't have time just to call in if we're leaving tonight so would you be able to put us up for the week-end?'

There was a slight pause.

Cindy frowned. 'Mum?'

'That man too, Cindy? I don't know . . .'

'Yes, Mum. Well, I can't talk now. We'll catch up on all the news when we get out there,' she interrupted quickly, forcing a cheerful note into her voice. 'We are leaving shortly so we'll be in time for dinner. Okay?'

'Okay, Cindy. We'll talk some more then. 'Bye for now.'

Slowly, Cindy hung up.

'It's all settled then?' Stuart asked.

'Yep! We're expected by dinner time.'

'Fine. Get your things packed and we'll get started right away.'

The view on the way out to Apiti was just as lovely as anything seen coming down from Auckland. The road twisted and turned its way up to Apiti and then up into the Ruahine Range to Hawai Farm and around each sharp bend, the rugged green country below them could be seen at dozens of different angles.

Cindy was silent throughout the drive, pretending to be intent on the scenery but in actual fact she was pondering over what her mother had said over the phone. What on earth made her jump to such a conclusion that her and Stuart? Why did she persist in saying 'that man' when referring to him and why was she so reluctant to have him stay with them for the week-end?

She sighed. 'I only hope Mum and Dad don't prove difficult or stand-offish if they don't like him and I'm sure Mum has already decided to dislike him. I just don't understand it.'

As they climbed from the car which Stuart parked up the long earth driveway of Hawai Farm, the cold air cut them to the marrow and Cindy grinned to herself as she heard Stuart utter softly: 'Holy hell!'

He took their two suitcases from the boot of the car and together they advanced towards the farmstead. It wasn't a big house but cosy and comfortable in a picturesque setting of a large garden harbouring trees, silver birches and cherry trees and a few sprawling wattle trees, all of which made a colourful splash during the spring and summer months.

'God, it's cold! Is this the fresh air you told me about?' Stuart asked, incredulously.

Cindy laughed, hugging herself against the cold.

'This is winter, remember.' She looked up at the sky. 'I think it'll be snowing before too long.'

'And I'll be frozen stiff before long.'

'Come on then. Let's hurry up and get inside. There's sure to be a fire going in the range and one in the living-room.' Walking on quickly she saw a tall lean figure striding through a clump of trees from the direction of the farm sheds.

Tony! Cindy's eyes lit up. 'Tony! Hey Tony!' she called and waved madly as he turned and saw them. Leaving Stuart's side she ran towards Tony and laughed exultantly as he caught her and whirled her around. 'Oh Tony,' she laughed breathlessly when he put her down. 'How are you?'

'Fine, and you?'

'Just great. Come and meet my boss, Mr. Newman.' She gestured to where Stuart had put down the two cases and was lighting up a cigarette. She sensed Tony's hesitation and glanced up at him. 'Come on.' Then she saw the expression on his face as he looked over at Stuart. It was vaguely frightening.

'Tony, what's wrong?'

'Wrong? Nothing's wrong, Cindy.' He smiled down at her. 'Come and introduce me to this boss of yours.'

Unconvinced, Cindy took him over and introduced the two men and saw Tony give Stuart an unfriendly stare and ignore his outstretched hand. 'Pleased to meet you,' he said curtly.

'What are you doing here, Tony?' Cindy asked quickly in an attempt to cover up his deliberate bad manners.

'We're expecting it to snow anytime now, so since Dad and I have finished loading up hay, I thought I'd come and give your father a hand.'

'That was good of you,' Cindy experienced a bewildered and angry kind of hurt at the rather cool way Tony was treating her and his rudeness to Stuart.

Almost without realizing it, she moved closer to Stuart as they went on into the house.

The same attitude towards Stuart was also adopted by both of her parents. They welcomed him formally enough but with forced politeness which riled her. She had never known them to treat any of her friends in such a manner and certainly not someone like Stuart, who held a position above her and had the power to dismiss her if he so wished.

'If we may be excused, I'll just show Stuart the guest room. I'm sure he would like to shower and unpack.' Cindy stood up and turned to Stuart who got up with lethargic ease and picked up his suitcase. Amusement glinted in his eyes and curved his mouth making her angrier than ever.

'What do you find so amusing?' she snapped when they were out of range of the kitchen.

'When you were going on about the marvellous attractions this place had to offer, you omitted to warn me about the rousing welcome one receives here. It was becoming pretty overpowering.' He grinned as he went past her into the guest room.

'There's no need to be sarcastic.'

He shrugged. 'I wasn't. I was just wondering what you wrote to them about me.'

'Do you really think that I consider you that important to include you in my letters?'

'Now who's being sarcastic?'

'Look, I'm sorry about all this and believe me I can't understand it. I never wrote anything about you in my letters.'

'Flatterer!'

'You'll find the bathroom the second door on your left!' She slammed the door shut and strode back out to the kitchen to where her mother was setting the table for dinner.

'Where's Dad and Tony?'

'Out in the washhouse cleaning up. Now Cindy, it's about time you and I had a talk . . .'

'That's for real! Do you realize that that was my boss you, Tony and Dad have just treated like — like something to be trodden on. Why, for crying out loud? You've all made me feel about this big!' She held up her hand, her forefinger and thumb about a half an inch apart.

'I'm sorry, we didn't want to . . .'

'Didn't want to? Then why did you?'

'Look, sit down and don't get so het up.'

With a sigh of exasperation, Cindy sat down and waited for her mother to explain.

'Did Jo and Keith go visiting last week-end? Putaruru for instance?'

'Why yes, how did you know?'

'My sister thought it her profound duty to ring and tell me the life story of my daughter's employer, the man she was also dating, the man who was the cause of her own daughter's heartbreak and misery, not to mention her bad name. She explained this Stuart Newman's character down to a T. Oh, I have no doubt that she coloured it up a little, but the fact still remains that you're working for and are dating some no-good who wouldn't hesitate to do the same to you that he has done to Jo.'

'I see,' Cindy said slowly. 'And do you think that because I may have gone out with him a few times, I also may have done certain things to earn myself a bad name?'

'Of course not! I trust you. Your father and I both do!' Beth Taylor was quick to retort. 'But you're very young and inexperienced and he is not so young and very experienced. He could try and sway you and quite against your will you could be swayed. The young are usually very impressionable.'

'Mum!' Cindy jumped to her feet, her face set. 'If you're wondering and worrying then let me assure

104

you that Stuart has not swayed me and if he tries, I'm not one who is easily swayed.' She studied her mother's face for a few seconds and saw the flicker of doubt in her eyes. 'You aren't convinced, are you? You still don't believe me?'

'Cindy,' her mother appealed, 'of course I believe you. It's just that I know the kind of man Stuart Newman is just by looking at him.'

'But Aunt Donna's colourful description did help, didn't it?'

'I do believe you!'

'Okay, okay. How did Tony know about Stuart? Don't tell me dear Aunt Donna thought it her duty to inform him also?'

'No, no,' Beth Taylor sighed wearily and sat down at the table. 'It was Fran.'

'Aunt Fran? Where does *she* fit in?'

'She was here when Donna rang . . .'

'Oh no! Go on.'

'Well, of course I had no idea what Donna was ringing about so it was natural that I should mention her name and that Fran should catch on to who it was. When Donna told me the danger you had placed yourself in I was shattered and confused. I tried to cover up the subject of the conversation, but Fran wanted to speak to her and so from what Donna told her and from what she had gathered herself, she knew the whole story.'

'And before you knew it the whole of this area knew about it and I subsequently end up with a bad reputation — and for nothing!' Cindy finished. 'How very amusing. I bet Aunt Fran was in her element of delight spreading the gossip and I bet she found even more enjoyment in telling Tony.'

'I'm sorry, but that's exactly what happened. That's Fran. Nothing ever went right for her from the start. A weak husband who drank too much and two children who got caught up with the wrong company. I

105

think they were the two biggest disappointments and worries in her life. She couldn't bear to see anyone else happy and especially not me. Not me with a loving husband and a lovely and loving daughter. "As pure as the driven snow," she had sneered at me after Donna had rung. I bet that snow isn't so pure now. I bet . . .'

'Oh!' Cindy shook her head and turned away, her hand hard over her mouth. 'And Tony — he believes her?' she whispered.

'He doesn't want to believe her.'

'But he does.'

'I didn't say that. He is confused. He doesn't know what to believe. However, the seed has been sown.'

'Oh, why did I come home? Why *did* I come home? Tony doesn't believe in me and even you don't really believe!' She threw down her hands, her palms facing upwards, then pausing only for a moment she rushed over to the door and pulled it open.

'Cindy — Cindy, where are you going?'

'Anywhere. To bed, to hell, anywhere rather than stay in here!'

'Your dinner . . .'

But the door slammed and Beth Taylor heard her daughter's footsteps running from the house.

The cold evening air cut through Cindy like a knife but she paid no heed. She ran on through the garden, down amongst the trees until she came to the orchard. Flinging herself down under the high spreading branches of a nectarine tree, where she had always sought consolation for her miseries as a child, she buried her head on her drawn-up knees and tried to relieve her feelings through tears, but none would come.

Finally she sat up, and with her arms hugging her knees, she gazed dry-eyed, unseeing and unthinking into nothingness.

'Ah, now that's a good sign. You're still running

away, but this time no tears. You're growing up, Cindy Taylor.'

Startled, she turned to find that Stuart was standing behind her. She lept to her feet and brushed her hands over the seat of her bright yellow slacks. 'No sign of tears isn't necessarily a sign of growing up!' she told him tersely, annoyed at this interruption.

'No, but it is a sign that you are learning that life isn't so rosy, perfect and beautiful and that you're beginning to accept it.'

'I can hardly not accept it, can I, when its imperfection and ugliness has been thrust up in front of me so much during the last month that I'm being choked with it! Anyway, how did you find me here?'

'Your mother told me what had been said and told me where I might find you.'

'Well, why didn't you just leave me alone — or do you always have to make a point of being present to witness me learning the facts of life?'

'Let's say I have a personal interest and a prize at stake,' he grinned.

Cindy had a vague recollection of having heard him use that particular word and meaning before; however, she was too angry to be bothered trying to figure out where. 'You just don't care that because of you my life here has virtually ended. People here who liked and respected me once will probably talk about me and cast me odd glances whenever I walk down the street.'

'Does Apiti have a street? It's probably so short and we probably went through it so fast that I didn't notice it.'

Cindy shook her head incredulously. 'I never really knew that people like you existed.'

'Come on now, honey, Apiti isn't the whole world. It's only a few hundred or so people.'

'It's my home, the people are my friends — or perhaps *you* didn't know such things existed. It just shows how ignorant even the most worldly people are; especially about the more important things in life.'

'When we get back to Auckland, I'll take you out to meet my mother.' His voice was harsh and his hand shot out to grasp her arm. He jerked her around to face him. 'And my home. Then we'll see just how ignorant I am about the "more important things in life",' he ended sarcastically.

Cindy felt such surprise at this that his last remark barely sank through to her. 'Your mother? I didn't know you had a mother.'

'Well, how do you think I came to be born — or did you think I just happened?'

'I'm sorry. What I meant was that I never thought of your parents as being alive. You never mentioned them.'

Stuart turned away impatiently, cursing himself for having mentioned his mother and in so doing, referring to his private life. It was a subject that he never spoke about to anyone, but now, in one reckless second, he had managed not only to arouse Cindy's interest and curiosity, but also to commit himself by promising to take her out to meet his mother.

'We'd better get back. Your folks will be wondering where we are and dinner will be getting cold.' He strode on ahead of her and wisely Cindy followed, not saying any more, controlling the urge to question him about his mother, what she was like and where she lived.

The next morning dawned cloudy and bleak. The snow had still managed to hold off although the air was bitterly cold.

Soon after lunch, when the temperature had risen a little, Cindy offered to show Stuart around the farm. She was sure that despite his constant bland, easy going expression and amicable manner, he would be thankful to escape from her parents' forced friendliness they still showed towards him.

'Can you ride?' Cindy asked.

'Yeah, I've done a bit in my time,' he replied as he tugged on a pair of her father's hefty boots.

Cindy began to laugh as they left the house and went in the direction of the farm sheds to get saddles and bridles for their horses. 'Boy, don't we look a pair of hard-cases? You look twice your size in those clothes of Dad's.' She took in the heavy leather boots and the old and stained, sheepskin lined leather hip-length jacket he wore. As usual he was bare headed, refusing her offer of one of her father's wide brim-med hats.

She was dressed similarly in blue jeans and heavy boots. She had a hat tied around her neck and rest-ing on the back of her equally old and stained jacket, just in case it rained or snowed while they were out.

Stuart grinned, eyeing her critically. 'So this is the real you. Dressed to look, not to mention smell, like a typical land girl.'

'Oh, shut up!' She tossed her head and lengthen-ing her stride she went ahead of him saying over her shoulder: 'The smell is clean and healthy.'

'I know. It's like you, so I've no objection,' he called, laughter in his voice.

She huffed in exasperation. She didn't think she altogether liked that, but she couldn't very well con-tradict herself so she ignored him, knowing that if she tried to put herself right he would inevitably twist everything she said until he got the better of her.

'Can you catch a horse for yourself?' Cindy panted, lugging a saddle and bridle from the shed and half staggering and half running to drape it over the fence.

'Sure,' he affirmed, effortlessly following her ex-ample and swinging a saddle over the fence next to hers.

'Right, which one do you want? The red one is Petra, she's mine, the dapple grey one is Poni, she's

Dad's and the other black one here in this paddock is Branded. He's the youngest and also the meanest. You can have whichever one you want.'

'I think Branded and I would make a swell pair. We sound alike. Two of a kind.'

Cindy laughed. 'Yeah, I think so too, but you'll have to catch him first. He's as cunning as he is mean and he can conquer even the highest fence. Sounds more and more like you, doesn't he?'

Stuart shot her a quick look before jumping down from the white gate on which they were sitting, into the paddock.

She watched as he took up the bridle and strode over to where the big black horse, a thoroughbred and a handsome one, was moving restlessly, his black eyes warily watching the approaching figure.

She saw the horse whinny protestingly as Stuart held out his hand. Then Branded moved back, having guessed Stuart's intention, and trotted to the far end of the paddock which dipped sharply and then rose steeply up the other side.

Suddenly, Cindy began to laugh, thoroughly enjoying it. Despite all Stuart's softly spoken words of persuasion, the horse clearly wasn't going to have any of it. And he too seemed to be finding enjoyment in having Stuart chase after him up and down the paddock.

She had learned from experience the frustration that Branded drove one to, when, the first time she had tried to catch him, he had leapt all the fences until he got on to the road. It had taken her the best part of the morning to round him up again.

Then she saw Stuart make a lunge at the horse after he had managed to corner him. Grabbing a handful of his black mane, Stuart slipped on the bridle and tried to lead the horse back across the paddock. But stubbornly, Branded refused to budge for a few seconds and then he gave a sudden whinny and reared back. As if prepared for this Stuart kept his hold on the reins and when the animal landed back on to its front hooves, he brought the reins up and whipped them across his black face. Startled, the horse quietened abruptly and at once became meek and obedient, but proud to go with it.

He stood quite still as Stuart leapt up on to his back and feeling Stuart's prodding kick at his sides, he galloped surefootedly down and up the sharp dip towards the saddles hanging on the fence.

'Well, do you still think the horse takes after you?' Cindy laughed as he brought the horse to a halt and slid down off his back. He was panting slightly with exertion.

Stuart swung the saddle up on to the horse's back, saying with his back facing her: 'No, in fact I think he takes after a certain female I know. He keeps backing back and running away even though he knows he can't escape getting caught in the long run.'

Cindy remained silent and jumped down from the gate on to the grass.

'Sorry about having to hit him,' Stuart went on as though he wasn't even expecting an answering jibe from her.

'Don't let that worry you. He's had a few beltings, especially from Dad. It's the only way you can get him to obey — by showing him just who's boss,' Cindy replied and immediately began to regret it, wondering what he would read into those remarks. She went on quickly:

'The trouble with Dad is that after he finally catches him he's so mad that he yells at him while he wallops him, using every swear word in the book and more, so the horse gets used to this and doesn't take any notice. He must have got a surprise when you only hit him.'

'Let me assure you that if you hadn't been within

shouting distance the horse would have heard a few words.'

Cindy laughed, tugging the bridle from the fence. 'Don't worry, that horse has heard his fair share from me,' she told him, thinking of the time when he had leapt all the fences leaving her yelling furiously after him.

She caught and saddled Petra without any trouble and together she and Stuart rode out through the gates into the Pump Paddock and on along the long track which curved around the steep hills out to the airstrip.

When they came to the boundary line of the farm which was marked by a wide clear flowing creek with trees lining its banks, they dismounted from their horses and strode through the long grass towards the steep descent of the hill leading to it.

A strong wind had now come up and was blowing through the trees, and across the paddocks so that they resembled miles of shining green silk.

Cindy lifted her face to the sky and frowned as she studied the low swollen clouds. 'Won't be long now,' she said, putting her hands up to keep back the strands of hair that had escaped from the pony-tail she had drawn back with a rubber band.

'Then let's enjoy all this grass while it's still with us,' Stuart suggested.

Cindy darted him a look and caught a glimpse of wicked invitation in his eyes, and bolted. 'Like hell,' she thought, and dodging past him, she began to run down the steep grassy slope. Glancing over her shoulder she saw him running close behind her.

She gave an excited, frightened laugh which broke off into a shriek as her heel slipped and shot from under her and landing with a thud on to her back, she rolled without stopping, and without being able to stop, to the bottom of the rugged hill giving a yelp every time she bounced over a jutting piece of earth.

Just as she was nearing the bottom she saw Stuart above her, rolling down perilously close to her. 'Stuart! You — you great idiot! You'll land on top of me!' she wailed, half laughing, then put her hands up to hold her head as if to protect herself.

When she stopped at last, she remained tense and still, her arms still cradling her head, waiting for Stuart's great weight to land on her.

But it didn't. Instead she felt a hand on her head and then sat up with an exclamation of surprise as Stuart tugged the rubber band from her hair.

'Now what did you go and do that for?' she demanded, glowering down into his laughing face.

He didn't answer. He took the rubber band and pulled it back across his thumb with his fingers and aimed it at her.

'Ow!' she cried, immediately ducking her head back into her arms and tensing herself against the stinging pain which, she suddenly realized, she hadn't yet felt.

'What are you owing for? The thing didn't even hit you,' Stuart laughed, folding his hands under his head.

'Well then, where is it?' she scowled, sitting up.

'It whizzed over your head. It could be anywhere. Shall we look for it together?' he said eagerly, propping himself up on to one elbow.

Cindy laughed helplessly and tugged a handful of grass and threw it in his face. 'You nut! Do you realize you could have squashed me rolling down there like that?'

'No?' He drew out the word with mocked wonder.

'Ohhh!' she muttered, exasperated. Pulling up another handful of grass, she rubbed some into his face and then jumping to her feet, her ankles out of reach of his hands, she dropped the rest on to the top of his head.

Instantly he was on his feet after her.

She shrieked, both terrified and excited at the same time. She turned and ran backwards, panting: 'Keep — keep away from me, Stuart Newman. I'm warning you. Just ke-keep away!'

'Okay.' Stuart slowed down and stopped, shrugging his broad shoulders.

Cindy stopped too and pushed back the hair which was covering her face, feeling relieved and yet strangely disappointed. She watched him warily, like she had seen the horse do, as he walked slowly towards her.

She stood rooted to the spot, incapable of moving, her eyes on his. When he reached her he encircled her wrists with his hands and drew her closer, gently until she was so close she could feel his breath on her face.

Her heart pounded as she realized that he was deliberately being gentle as if repenting for his wild ruthlessness before. While she wanted more than anything to lift her face to his, something within her held her back and made her remain rigid and unresponsive.

'Cindy.' Stuart bent his head to hers and instantly she turned away. He didn't move. 'I'm not forcing you this time,' he told her, watching her profile.

'I realize that.'

'Is it because of what your mother said?'

She tried to free her hands so as to smooth back her hair, but Stuart retained his hold on her wrists so she shook her hair back from her face instead. She looked up at him. 'No, not necessarily. It's what has happened because of what she knows, because of what she thinks has happened between us, and Tony . . .'

'Tony?' Stuart's eyes narrowed.

Cindy nodded. 'He has heard too, that's why he was so unfriendly to you and so cold to me. I've got to get a chance to explain to him that there was and is nothing between us.'

'*Got* to?'

Cindy nodded again, and looked away.

'Why?'

'Because Tony and I have an — understanding. I can't bear to have him think bad of me.'

'Understanding?'

'Tony wanted to marry me before I left. Everyone wanted us to marry, his parents and my parents. Dad wanted us to marry because having no son, his only heir a daughter, he thought there would be nothing better than if we married and when the Maxwells and Mum and Dad decided to retire then the two farms could merge and become a station. But I didn't want to settle down without getting around a bit first.'

'And so you were going to come back here and marry that young smart alec when you had had your fling?' Stuart released her wrists and moved away from her.

'That was what I didn't know. I didn't know whether I wanted to settle down here and marry Tony. I didn't know whether I loved Tony enough.'

'And do you know yet?'

Cindy lied silently by shaking her head and then followed him as he turned away and began climbing up the hill to where they had left the horses.

Later that night Apiti's surrounding farm districts experienced their first snow fall of the season and by morning nearly everything in sight was glistening white under a rising sun.

George Taylor was dressed and ready for breakfast early that morning, wanting to get an early start on doing his rounds of the farm and throwing out hay for his stock which he had rounded up and kept in sheds or to the lower levels of the farm.

Stuart was up early too and made an offer to give him a hand, and Cindy quickly intervened before her father had a chance to refuse. 'If you'd really like to go, Dad would welcome a hand, wouldn't you, Dad?'

George Taylor gave a grunt and getting to his feet he turned to address Stuart: 'Well, if you're coming you'd better get mobile. I'll be leaving just as soon as I've fetched my knife and boots from the wash-house. I don't suppose you've got any gloves?'

'No, sir.'

'No, then I'll get you a pair of mine you can wear,' he said grudgingly. 'Don't forget to bring the flask of coffee when Beth has made it.'

Before he left, Stuart told Cindy to have her things packed and ready for they would be leaving just as soon as he returned.

At about two o'clock that afternoon, Stuart and George Taylor had still not returned and Cindy was just about to ring Tony for the second time that day to see if he was in, when she saw him through the living-room window coming up the drive on horse-back.

'I'll be back in a minute, Mum,' she called and rushed out to meet him.

She waited at the top of the drive for him to reach her. 'Hi, Tony.'

'Hi. Mum said you telephoned this morning. You wanted to speak to me?'

'Uh huh,' Cindy affirmed, nodding her head. Nervously she ran the tip of her tongue over her lips. 'I hope I didn't drag you away from your work.' She gave him what she hoped was a bright smile.

'You didn't,' he said briefly, not returning her smile. 'What did you want to speak to me about?'

Cindy sighed, realizing that she wasn't reaching him. It was almost as if she was talking to a stranger instead of someone she had known all her life. 'Tony, why are you so cold to me — acting as if I were a stranger?' she blurted. 'You never used to be like this. Before I left . . .'

'A lot of water has flowed under the bridge since then, Cindy.'

She stiffened. 'Meaning?'

'Surely you know what I mean. Hasn't your mother told you that she knows and I know about that — that tycoon-Galahad?'

'He does have a name, Tony. And just what *do* you know about Stuart and me?'

'I'm trying to spare you any unnecessary embarrassment . . .'

'Spare me any embarrassment?' she echoed, dumbfounded. 'Why should I be embarrassed about anything? Just because Aunt Donna happened to ring up and tell Mum, Stuart Newman's past life doesn't necessarily mean . . .' She stopped, seeing the cold way in which Tony was regarding her. 'You don't mean to say you believe all that guff Aunt Fran told you about Stuart and me?' she said incredulously.

'Look, Cindy, I've got to get back. Dad's expecting me to help him to clear the snow away from the drive so that he can get the car out.'

'Just one darn minute!' Cindy caught at his arm and with strength she didn't know she had, she swung him around as he went to mount his horse. 'I asked you a straight question and I want a straight answer. Do you believe that Stuart and I have been having an — affair?'

'Well, haven't you?'

She released her hold on his arm and stepped back and Tony mounted his horse.

'I see. It wouldn't make any difference if I denied it, would it? You have already made up your mind.'

'No, I haven't. I just don't know what to think. I'm confused and God knows I'm that blasted wild I could knock Newman's block off his shoulders. I loved you, Cindy and I trusted you. I wanted to marry you. But you've changed and the circumstances have changed, even I can see that. And perhaps I've changed too. Why did you have to leave here? Why couldn't you have just been happy to remain here — as my wife?' He swung his horse around and giving him a kick with his heels, he started into a gallop down the long drive lined with naked silver birch trees.

'Oh, go ahead and believe what you damn well please!' she shouted after him and watching him go, she pressed her knuckles against her teeth and bit into them hard. Suddenly, she turned on her heel and ran back to the house. 'Perhaps the next time I see all of you, I'll have done something to justify your beliefs.'

She changed into a charcoal grey slack suit and an ice-blue under-jumper, then with deft, automatic movements she flung all her belongings into the suitcase lying open on her bed and clicked it shut and stood looking about her at the room she had occupied for the best part of twenty years.

She started visibly as Stuart's voice spoke to her from the doorway. 'Are you all packed and ready?'

She turned and saw his rugged face and his eyes, glowing healthily from the hard, strenuous work outdoors. His clothes were dirty and a bit torn and his hair was flattened against his forehead by the wind.

'Yes, yes, I'm ready. Her voice was vague. 'Please hurry, I want to leave. Now. As soon as possible.'

CHAPTER SIX

IT SEEMED like six hours instead of only one before the snow was cleared from the drive and they were finally on their way, travelling at a steady pace along the highway which had been cleared of snow earlier that day.

'God, I'm hungry! Farm work gives a man one almighty appetite.' Stuart muttered contentedly.

'Here, I made some sandwiches and hot chocolate. I thought you might be hungry seeing as you were too late for lunch.' Cindy sorted around in her shoulder bag for a pack of mutton sandwiches and opened it on the seat beside him.

'Great. You're an angel — the backblocks variety.' He threw her a grin and bit into one of the sandwiches.

Feeling horribly close to tears, she quickly turned her head away from him and stared at the country, now only scattered lightly with snow and sleet as they travelled down and out of the Ruahine Range. She couldn't cry now in front of him. She needed sympathy, not another lecture on: 'This is life — stand up and face it,' which was exactly what she did get as soon as he guessed her inner turmoil of emotion.

'They say a place is never the same once you have gone away and left it.'

'I should never have gone back.'

'Well, we all learn by our mistakes. You're only one of many.'

Cindy gritted her teeth and blinked back the tears furiously. 'Do you always have to be indifferent about everything?' she asked tightly, the view becoming blurry and out of focus.

'It doesn't pay to get involved in other people's private affairs or emotional entanglements!' he snapped irritably. 'They only repay you with a smack in the eye if you try to help them out. That you'll learn too. And if you're going to sit there blubbering all afternoon, then I'm damn sure I'm not going to sit here listening to you or sit here talking to myself!' With that he leaned over and switched on the car radio and listened to the music on whichever station he was able to get.

It was about nine-thirty when they at last approached the suburbs of Auckland. Most of the distance had been travelled in silence — during which Cindy had huddled up against the car door and slept fitfully. Now, yawning, she uncurled from her cramped position and stretched her legs straight out in front of her, half closing her eyes against the glare of the city and approaching car lights.

'What time is Jo expecting you home?' Stuart asked.

Not looking at him, Cindy shrugged and leaned over to clear the windows which were beginning to mist over.

'Then do you feel like going out somewhere for something to eat?'

'We're hardly dressed for that. Anyway, won't your housekeeper be expecting you?'

'I doubt whether Elizabeth will be back from her holiday yet.'

'In that case, I'll cook you something.'

Stuart darted a look at her. 'At my place?'

'Well, I can hardly cook it up in the middle of Auckland's Harbour Bridge,' Cindy retorted, her tone hard and her expression set. 'What are you looking at me like that for? I thought you were hungry.'

'So I am, but . . .'

'Jo and Keith won't be expecting me at any set time if that's what you're worried about.'

Stuart swung his car off the main highway in the direction of his home situated a little out from the city. He studied Cindy's profile covertly. Her expression, uncertain and yet defiant, her chin thrust out. She shook back her tumbled hair and curled her legs up on the seat once more. Resting the side of her jaw on her hand, her wide eyes stared out of the window unseeingly. Stuart knew that already she was half regretting her impulsive suggestion, feeling that she had in some way committed herself, to what though, she wasn't too sure.

All her actions from then on were decisive with a touch of finality to them. She shut the car door with a bang and swung the coat of her slack suit over her shoulder and stood tapping her foot impatiently while she waited for Stuart to collect his suitcase from the boot of the car.

She shivered a little, listening to the cool breeze whistling eerily through the many huge trees surrounding the grounds. It seemed to be warning her as Jo had done, telling her to go, to get away before it was too late. But already it was too late, Stuart was holding out his arm to her and putting it gently against her shoulders, he led her into the house.

She couldn't control her shivering now as the cold dark interior of the house greeted them. Stuart switched on the hall lights. 'You look frozen stiff. Come into the lounge. I'll set the fire. This house is like an ice-box.'

Cindy followed him into the lounge and watched him set the fire in the same fire grate she had sat in front of the first night they had met. The photo of Delia which he had smashed so violently and then burned had not been replaced by another.

'Do you still want to cook dinner?' Stuart asked, standing up and wiping his dusty hands on the thighs of his already dirty jeans.

'Of course,' Cindy replied flippantly, flinging her bag and jacket into a nearby chair.

He frowned a little at her unusual careless manner and lack of enthusiasm for what she was doing.

'Come on then, I'll show you where things are kept and then I'll go and have a shower and change seeing as I didn't have time to before I left.'

In other circumstances, Cindy would have found joy in cooking in Stuart's kitchen for it was equipped with every modern convenience, all of which were within hand's reach. The stove was quick and the frying pans and saucepans were nonstick and easy to wash. But as it was, Cindy felt nervous and apprehensive, wondering what she was letting herself in for, but determined not to back out.

She jumped every time she heard a floor board creak or a piece of cutlery slip from the bench into the sink or on to the floor and finally she jerked down the venetian blinds to cover the wide windows which during the day time would allow the sun to fill the room, but at that moment were reflecting her shadow and every movement so that she started violently each time she saw herself move or heard the trees' branches outside knock softly against the glass.

When at last she had the meal set out on to two plates, she placed them on a tray together with knives and forks and pepper and salt and carried it carefully into the lounge. Even though she was expecting to see Stuart coming through the door of the lounge, her heart still leapt with fright, making her hands holding the tray, tremble dangerously.

Stuart quickly relieved her of the tray and set it on the low coffee table near the fire.

'What's the matter with you? You're terrifically jumpy. You'll be jumping at your own shadow next.' He threw several cushions on to the floor in front of the fire, and sat down.

'That's exactly what I have been doing. It's so dark and spooky outside and I could see every movement I made in those blasted windows out in the kitchen.' Cindy sat down on the cushions beside him and handed him his plate. 'When are you expecting your house-keeper back?'

'Elizabeth? Tomorrow probably.'

'She seems to be pretty efficient.'

'She is. I don't know what I'd do without her.'

'What about when you get married?'

Stuart seemed to choke over a piece of steak. He turned to look at her. 'Are you trying to be funny?'

'Of course not. You'll probably get married some-day in spite of your present outlook.'

'Honey, I've learned my lesson where women are concerned and while it was very educational it wasn't at all pleasant or an experience I'd like to repeat. As you know, I'm a guy who learns by his mistakes.'

'Of course,' she agreed demurely. When she had finished eating, she placed her empty plate down on the tray and getting to her feet, she wandered over to the radiogram and began sorting through the pile of records. She chose one entitled 'Angel' and set it spinning on the turn-table.

She swayed to the music for a few moments and then held her hands out to Stuart, who taking his time, stood up and drew her into his arms.

As they danced slowly to the music, Cindy could smell the freshness of Taboc soap clinging to him. He smelled clean and even felt clean right through the green wool of his skivvie. Boldly she looked up at him and said: 'But what if you did fall in love — with anyone — with me even?'

His eyes narrowed as he saw the unfamiliar hard brilliance of hers and her mouth set in lines displaying her feeling of recklessness. She had been hurt terribly. Stuart could see that, and he could also see that she was determined to hit back in any way she was able, whether it be according to or against her high ideals.

'That would be most unlikely,' he said. 'If I desired you then I'd love you well. That is the only love I'm capable of, but while it lasted it would be wonderful and exciting and you'd never regret a moment.' He spoke slowly and intensely, his eyes holding hers. His head lowered and then Cindy felt his lips on hers, and at their contact she felt her heart race wildly with a mixture of both terror and ecstasy. Gradually she relaxed, recklessly determined to surrender to the sharp sweet pain caused by her heart turning within her.

Stuart lifted his head only to murmur: 'Lord, hasn't he ever kissed you before? You've got a lot to learn.'

She opened her eyes and looked straight up into his and caught sight of the laughter there and also something else she was unable to define.

He drew her down on to the cushions on the floor. She sensed the change in him. His kisses seemed to contain a certain amount of anger and ruthlessness as did his hands pinioning her shoulders. The strength in him frightened her.

She tried to wriggle free but couldn't. Then it struck her that right this minute she was merely another woman to him, just another of the countless number of women in his life.

Upon realizing this her desire to hit back, which from the beginning had mounted slowly and had grown stronger, petered out abruptly. She knew that she didn't want to be just 'another woman' to him, and this was worth more than anything, even his hate. She struggled, pushing at him with her hands and turning her head to avoid his kisses, panting at him to let her go.

'No!'

'Let me up!'

'Why should I?' He lifted his head, his eyes dark and brilliant, looked scornfully into hers. 'This is what you wanted, isn't it? It's certainly what you've been asking for so, baby, you're getting it!'

'No!' She turned her head frantically.

'Why? Would you rather it was Tony?' he snarled. 'Look at me!' Putting his finger under her chin he twisted her face around to his. 'But it wouldn't be Tony, would it? It'll never be Tony now. He believes what your aunt told him and so do your parents. They say they don't, but underneath they have their doubts. You're angry and hurt and want to hit back and I present the excellent opportunity. You were going to use me as a means of hitting back. Isn't that true?'

Cindy opened her mouth to protest.

'Isn't that true?' Stuart repeated angrily.

'Oh, okay then, yes, yes, yes! That's what you wanted to hear, isn't it? Are you satisfied?'

He laughed mirthlessly. 'Far from it. And now you want to back out, eh? Too bad you're at my mercy, isn't it?'

'Yes, isn't it, when you haven't got any?'

Threateningly he made a move towards her, then flinging her aside, he said: 'I may not have any, but I have no desire to make love to someone like you who not only uses a man but also commits herself to him and then backs down, pleading for mercy. Just remember in future that I dislike being used. You may not get off so lightly next time.' He got to his feet and roughly pulled her up with him. 'And I'd advise you to watch whom you try those tactics on or you might find yourself in more trouble than you bargained for.'

With a muffled sob caused by the pain in her arm after his rough handling, she brought her other arm up and landed the flat of her palm across his face, with all her strength behind it.

She watched as his dark skin reddened. She knew that it must have hurt but he didn't move a muscle. His eyes merely regarded her steadily and with cold dislike.

'Here's your jacket and bag.' He threw the jacket to her and dropped the bag at her feet. 'I'll run you home.'

'Well, I'd have rather had his hate and now I've got it,' she thought dejectedly as Stuart drove her home. He pulled up and waited for her to get out but somehow she felt she couldn't leave him without saying something.

'Stuart,' she said tentatively in a low voice.

He didn't answer. He sat staring ahead of him with both his arms resting on the wheel.

'It was just as you said,' she began haltingly. 'I wanted to hit back at the folks back home and I thought that by doing the things they suspected me of I would feel justified, but then I suddenly realized that revenge would be meaningless — futile somehow . . .' She paused. 'Stuart, won't you say something? I'm sorry. I really am sorry.'

Still he wouldn't answer.

Cindy sighed. 'I mean it — it wasn't as if you loved me or would ever love me. Afterwards I would have hated myself — like you hate me now. At least I still have my self-respect and pride, a little battered perhaps, but it's all I've got and I intend to keep it.

'Well, aren't you going to say anything?' she cried after a lengthy pause.

'What is there to say? You have had quite an eventful evening in more ways than one. You deliberately led me on and then retreated, slapped my face and polished the whole thing off with a carefully worded speech in which you both excused yourself and apologized at the same time. There's nothing for me to add, is there?' he said coldly. 'You've managed

126

to round it off very nicely. Good-night — and don't bother coming to work tomorrow!'

Cindy blinked back tears of hopelessness. 'Why? Are you giving me notice?'

'Why the hell should I give you notice? You're a fine secretary if nothing else. It's just that I've had a gutsful of you, enough to last me a good while. If you feel you must come to work then make sure you keep out of my way. Type out those reports you have with you. Anything, but I don't want to lay eyes on you.' He reached over and swung the door open. 'Come on, get out.'

On Monday, Cindy did as he said and kept well out of his way. She could tell that he still hadn't cooled down by the sharp way he spoke to her when she put through his telephone calls. However, by the time Wednesday came he was a little more civil, but only speaking to her when he wished her to take down his dictation.

That afternoon, she was surprised to see Paul Brent enter her office. 'Hi, honey. Still with us, eh? My, you're lasting out a long time — longer than the others, that is.'

Cindy smiled her greeting. 'What do you mean by that?'

'His secretaries.'

'Oh, that.' She laughed. 'I have no doubt that it won't be long before he really flies off the handle and sacks me. If you ask me I think his other secretaries left of their own free will. I can't imagine many who would weather his hot-tempered pigheadedness for too long.' Immediately she was appalled at her definite unfairness and lack of loyalty to her boss. 'I'm sorry, I shouldn't have said that.'

Paul laughed. 'Don't worry. I won't tell him that he has another secretary who is madly in love with him,' he assured her confidently.

Cindy's eyes narrowed; however, she chose to ignore his remark. 'Do you wish to speak to Mr. Newman?'

'I do, but I'd much rather speak with you.' He rested his hands on her desk and leaned forward.

'I'm sorry but I just haven't the time. I'm very busy.' Nevertheless, unable to resist his infectious grin she picked up the telephone receiver and rang through to Stuart's office. 'Paul Brent to see you,' she answered Stuart's irritable: 'What is it?'

'Oh, what the hell does he want? Send him in!'

'You'd better go in. He doesn't sound in a very bright mood,' Cindy grimaced, jerking the telephone away from her ear as Stuart slammed the receiver down.

'And if I'm guessing right, he'll be in an even worse one when I leave,' Paul told her cheerfully, winking at her.

Shrugging, she turned back to her typing, quite blissfully unaware of what was going on between Paul and Stuart at that precise moment.

'Now, what do *you* want?' Stuart snapped impatiently. 'And for Pete's sake take that ridiculous grin off your face. It sickens someone who works all day for a living.'

'You don't have to slave away like you do and you know it.' Paul hitched his slacks and sprawled out in a chair. 'Besides, I'm on holiday now, remember?'

'Yeah, yeah — well, say what you have to say and then get.' Stuart looked at his watch. 'The day is nearly over and I don't seem to be getting any work done.'

Paul raised an eyebrow. He searched in his pocket for his cigarettes and offered the pack to Stuart. 'Mmm, Cindy was right, you are in a foul mood.'

Stuart's face darkened. 'So, I'm in a foul mood,

that doesn't explain what you're here for!' He put the cigarette between his lips, picked up a file from his desk and peered at the name written on it. Getting to his feet he searched through the filing cabinet, dropped it in and slammed the drawer shut.

'Cindy.'

Stuart looked at him impatiently.

'Have you forgotten? It's nearing the end of the month and I've come to collect. We may as well start making our arrangements now.'

'Well, I've got news for you, buddy boy, I'm pulling out.'

'You've still got a few more days before you're licked.'

'Maybe you didn't click. I've just pulled out, finished, quit! The bet was a lousy one anyway.'

'You mean you're already licked?'

'Sure I mean I'm licked. That — that crazy female out there doesn't know whether she's coming or going. She's too young to know her own mind.'

'That hasn't stopped you in the past.'

'Well, it has now. I'm sick to death of it. Sick to death of women and what they stand for. Just give me my peaceful bachelor existence — big game fishing in the Bay of Islands, fishing in the rivers and lakes and hunting in the bush. . . . Well, how about it, Paul? Time off to go hunting and fishing in the spring?'

'Fallen for that dumb, mixed up female out there?'

Stuart laughed, shoving another file into the drawer of the cabinet. 'Come off it, you know me better than that!'

'Yeah,' Paul eyed him sceptically. 'Well, anyway, you still owe me so we will go on that hunting trip . . .'

'I called it off!'

'Only because you knew it was hopeless.'

'Only because I realize that it was a rotten bet. I'm a rat and I know it, but I doubt if even a rat would sink so low. When we go on this trip we go for the sport, not because of any bet, okay?'

'Okay, but you're not forgetting that stag head by any chance?'

'To hell with the stag head! It wouldn't have been an entirely satisfying prize anyway, knowing that it was you who hunted it down. This time it'll be me. Stuart grinned suddenly and punched his friend on the side of his shoulder. All at once he felt a weight lift from him. He felt happier and carefree. He wouldn't allow himself to dwell too long on the question: 'Why?' Perhaps, inwardly, he was afraid of what the answer might be and what it would mean.

Cindy was surprised and puzzled, but happily so, at the abrupt change in Stuart's mood. He stopped at her desk on Thursday morning and told her that if she would like it he would arrange for them to spend the weekend with his mother who lived some distance out of Auckland.

'He wants you to *what?*' Jo exclaimed when she heard.

'He wants me to spend the week-end with him and his mother,' Cindy repeated patiently.

'But I never knew he had a mother — alive, I mean.'

'Neither did I. He let it slip accidentally during one of our many heated arguments. He promised me then that he would take me to meet her. I think he is only inviting me because of that.'

Jo could only stare at Cindy. This was a side of Stuart that she did not know and hadn't glimpsed at before. 'It's almost incredible,' she thought, thinking back on the rakish loner she had once known, and with whom she fell painfully in love. He had never mentioned his past and had brilliantly avoided ever discussing the subject when it had been brought up.

'Do you mind if I go?' Cindy was asking.

'I don't know. I just don't know.' Jo sat down, wearily pushing her hair back from her face. 'Is he fair dinkum?'

'I think so. In fact — yes, I'm positive he is. Jo, I would like to go.'

'I can't stop you, Cindy.'

'I know, but I'd feel a lot happier if you had no objection. I know you and Keith weren't too keen on me travelling down to Palmy with him, but there was really nothing to be worried about.'

Jo gestured with her hands and lifted her shoulders. 'Well then, there's not much to be said, is there, except that it looks as though he's changed. Incredible though it seems, to me at any rate.'

Impulsively, Cindy bent and kissed her cousin and laughed gaily, for the first time, Jo realized, since she had come back from visiting her family in Apiti and told her of the disruption unwittingly caused by her mother.

'Dear Jo. Thank you — thanks a lot. I feel a lot happier now.'

'You sound very jubilant. Is it just this proposed trip to see Stuart's mother — or because you've fallen for Stuart and are looking forward to a week-end almost alone with him?'

The gaiety drained from Cindy's face.

'Have I hit the nail on the head then?' Jo asked quietly.

'No — no! I don't love him. I can't, for there would be no future in that, only pain. You said so yourself.'

'I know what I said, honey, but that wouldn't stop you falling in love with him. I warned you of that too, in not so many words. I warned you not to learn by your own experience but to take my advice.'

Cindy turned away, clenching her hands. 'I won't admit it! I won't! Why, sometimes I hate the very sight of him.'

Jo sighed. 'It happens like that to all of us — with Stuart. Watch you don't end up like us, that's all.'

On Saturday, Stuart appeared more relaxed than Cindy had ever known him to be, casually dressed in dark slacks and red short sleeved shirt and lounging behind the wheel of his car.

They travelled at a steady pace which rapidly increased as they approached the country highways. It was barely eight o'clock in the morning but it was as clear and sunny as any midsummer's day.

Stuart drove with one hand on the wheel and with the elbow of one brown arm leaning on the open window. He switched on the car radio and sang softly to the music, every now and then looking at her and flashing a lazy smile.

His singing was pleasant to listen to and as the sun's rays found their way into the car, dappling his face and bare arms, emphasizing their darkness, Cindy found herself completely absorbed.

'You can do it really well,' she complimented him. 'Tell me about your mother. What is she like?'

Immediately his expression hardened into its more familiar lines. 'You'll see. I'm afraid we don't hit it off too well so don't expect to see a tearful mother rush out to greet her one and only son with a loving embrace, or expect to join in or listen to us chatter about what has happened since our last meeting, because it won't be like that. Whenever we meet, which isn't that often, we're either at each other's throat or we sit in silent enmity. Just a warning so that you'll know what to expect, for she won't put on an act just for your benefit.'

Cindy was surprised at this, then became aware of a sinking feeling of disappointment, and even disbelief. However, she soon discovered that what Stuart had told her was the truth.

They found Kiri Newman reclining back in a cane chair on the patio of her home, with her feet up, and leafing through a pile of magazines.

It was a lovely bungalow facing Muriwai Beach where from the patio, one could see the wide, deserted expanse of blue sea and pale sands. The bungalow was virtually the only one for miles, lonely and quiet and surrounded by rugged country.

The garden itself was vast and well kept and dipped slowly down towards the beach. It was almost empty of flowers, except for a few wild flowering shrubs which forced their way through and around native bushes, ferns and punga trees and several other huge trees that would prove to be adequate and welcome shade during the summer.

Kiri Newman looked up from the magazine on her slack-clad lap as she heard Stuart and Cindy's footsteps climbing the steps of the patio. She took off her glasses and leaning her elbow on the arm of the chair, she chewed at the end of her glasses as she watched them approach. 'You're early, aren't you?' she greeted Stuart discouragingly.

'Well, try not to sound so pleased to see me,' Stuart answered, turning to introduce Cindy.

Cindy was aware of the woman's cold eyes sweep her from head to foot as though she was summing up some old item of furniture, wondering whether or not to cast it out on to the rubbish heap.

'Huh! Another of your conquests?' she said at last, looking at Stuart. 'I've never known you to bring any of them here before.'

There was a slight uncomfortable silence. Then, 'Do you have to, Mother?' Stuart drawled finally.

Kiri Newman merely laughed scornfully. She turned to Cindy. 'Did you hear that? Talk about the pot calling the kettle black. Since when did you adopt for yourself the role of a saint?' she asked Stuart.

'I was thinking of Cindy. It's embarrassing for her to hear you talk so degradingly.'

She swore in awed tones. 'Say, you have got it bad!' she laughed loudly.

Cindy's eyes widened. As Stuart had said, she was feeling embarrassed, and sorry — for him. How painful it must be for him to have to introduce this hard woman as his mother. A mother who held nothing but scorn and contempt for her only son. It was expressed clearly in her cold blue eyes every time she looked at him. 'If this is how the week-end is going to continue, then it isn't going to prove to be much fun for any of us,' Cindy thought.

Looking over at Stuart she saw the anger, and — was it disappointment? — written there. Suddenly she sensed his desire to be alone with his mother. Quickly, she said: 'I'll just go and collect my belongings from the car.'

Stuart nodded and Cindy hurriedly took off down the patio steps.

'Well, she's a change from Delia, isn't she? Innocent as they come by the look of her. Huh, she won't stay that way if she's around you for too long,' Kiri laughed.

'For God's sake, shut up!' Stuart snapped, his eyes blazing with anger. He went on quietly, but not very evenly: 'I rang up the other day to tell you that I'd be coming and that I'd be bringing Cindy. I asked you and you gave me your word that you'd try to be as *charming* and as *pleasant* as possible,' he stressed the words sneeringly, 'as it was possible for you to be, that is. I especially asked you to promise me this one favour, the only favour I've asked of you in my whole life, and what do you do? Deliberately go back on your word, loving every minute of it!'

Kiri took no notice of her son's anger, instead she bit pensively on her glasses. 'Did I give you my word?

I can't remember. Funny. I must have forgotten.'

Stuart shook his head slowly.

'Oh, hell!' Kiri went on relentlessly. 'What's so terribly tragic about what's just happened? If she throws you over just because you have a mother like me, then let her go. You're fine and handsome, or so you appear to the opposite sex, so charming and rugged, like your god-damned father, you'll find someone else. You always have.'

'Don't speak to me like that about my father!' Stuart flared swiftly, turning to face his mother. 'You left him. Don't always try to relieve your own guilt by taking it out on me. You were the one at fault, not my father and not me. Why must you hate me just because I remind you of him? When are you going to accept your guilt and stop endeavouring to find excuses for what you've done? Can't you see me as a son and not a replica of my father, a replica of your hatred for my father . . .? Oh, what's the use?'

'What has got you feeling sorry for yourself all of a sudden?' she asked, looking up from a studious inspection of her nails.

'Could it be a perfectly normal yen for the affection which I've never had?'

'Affection?' Kiri laughed as if the idea of Stuart yearning for affection was hilarious as well as ridiculous. 'That's something you'll never lack, my fine son, even from that young thing you've brought here with you. Just lavish on the famous charm. . . .'

'I meant maternal affection.'

'Maternal affection?' Kiri echoed. 'Oh, come on, Stuart, I'm not such a fool as all that. You and I, we know each other too well to know it couldn't be that.'

'I don't think we know each other at all. You never gave us the chance to know each other really

135

well, or form a real warm relationship between us.'

'That's a lie!' Kiri leapt to her feet at this. Her eyes, now void of all sarcasm and scorn, were as blazingly angry as her son's. 'How dare you speak to me like that! I've had to bring you up alone for seven years until you were twenty-one. I did my best, but you needed a man whose firm hand could stop you from taking the path you took. I wasn't strong enough to do it alone. Every time I tried you'd turn on me because I had left your father. I wasn't strong enough to take that either. No mother wants her son's hate and I doubt whether any mother could stand it. However, I am still your mother and I'm still worthy of your respect.'

Stuart seemed to hesitate, then suddenly turned his back on her. Cindy, who had witnessed Stuart's action of finality, was standing perfectly still at the top of the patio steps. She saw the stricken face of Kiri Newman, white to the lips and aged years within the space of a few seconds. Her slim figure in bright blue slacks and paler blue sweater, tautened and her hands clenched themselves at her sides.

Stuart made for the steps, paused in his stride for a few seconds at seeing Cindy standing there, and then without a word he brushed passed her, down the steps and across the stretch of sloping lawn towards the beach.

A painful lump lodged in her throat as she looked after him, then to his mother. Suddenly, she turned to go after him when she was stopped by Kiri's slightly hysterical husky voice.

'You fool! Leave him. He's not worth it. He has always been like this and always will. You'll never change him.'

'I have no wish to, Mrs. Newman.' Cindy looked back and then started down the steps.

Kiri ran to the railings and leaned over. 'So you're

in love with him, eh? You poor fool. It'll do you no good. He'll never love you. He's never loved anybody, not even himself, and he never will.'

'I'm sorry, Mrs. Newman, really I am, but I must go. I can't just — just let him go,' Cindy shouted back.

'When someone doesn't love even himself, how can he have any love for others!'

'No, I don't believe that! How can you say something like that about your own son?'

'Because he is my son, and I know what he's capable of more than you do.'

Cindy turned from her, a shiver shuddering through her. With her hair flying out behind her, she ran across the grass and half ran and half slipped down the scattering of rocks on to the sand of the beach. 'Stuart! Stuart, wait for me!' she shouted breathlessly. 'Please!' But Stuart's tall figure ahead of her neither paused to look around, nor stopped.

Too breathless to run any more over the soft sands which impeded her progress, she flopped down on to a huge black bark of tree which had been washed up by the sea on to the beach, and waited until she could catch her breath.

She shivered despite the fact she was hot both from running and the penetration of the warm winter sun.

She shook her head, trying to get Kiri Newman's words out of her mind, but unwillingly she found her mind would keep recalling them. 'So you're in love with him, eh? You poor fool! It'll do you no good. He'll never love you. He's never loved anybody, not even himself and he never will . . .'

Cindy ran the tip of her tongue over her lips and swallowed dryly. She felt miserable and at a loss as to what to do, or how to act for the best. Finally she got to her feet and roamed along the beach, picking up various kinds of shells, inspecting them and then dropping them again.

What a start to what she thought was going to be a wonderful week-end. Privileged because Stuart was taking her to meet his mother, something he had never done before with any other woman. And now, she thought, she could understand why. Now, she thought she could understand a lot of things, or at least understand them more than she could before. But there was still a lot to be explained before she could understand fully the reason for Stuart's ruthless cruelty, his hardness and disillusionment.

At last, when the sun had risen far into the sky, telling her that it must surely be way past lunch time, she turned and reluctantly headed for the bungalow once more. However, before she reached the foot of the rocks lined along the bottom of the elevated grounds leading up to the bungalow, she saw Stuart coming down towards her carrying something in his hands.

She stopped and waited for him to reach her, surprised to find him coming from that direction, for she was positive he couldn't have passed her when he doubled back.

'Mother has gone to bed with a headache,' he told her briefly. 'I've brought some food and coffee for lunch. I hope you don't mind if we have it here on the beach.'

Cindy shook her head and sat down with him on the sand. In silence he unwrapped cellophane packages and handed her a bread roll and mug for her coffee. She took them without looking up.

'What else have you got in there?' she nodded to the knapsack still tightly packed.

'Our swimming gear. I thought you might like to go in for a quick swim. The water will probably be 'pretty bracing, but the sun's warm enough,' he answered tonelessly.

'But I didn't bring my bathing suit.'

'I know. I've brought you one I found up at the bungalow.'

'Delia's no doubt,' Cindy thought dully.

The silence dragged on and Stuart made no mention of what had happened back at the bungalow.

'It's weird,' Cindy thought. Desperately she tried to think of something to say, but whenever she opened her mouth to say whatever had come into her mind, she closed it again, realizing how silly it would sound. She was afraid too, that her voice would come high-pitched caused by nervous tension.

She forced herself to eat and gulped down her mug of hot coffee.

Stuart sat, his expression brooding and distant, every now and then inhaling at the smoking cigarette held between his fingers.

At last he reached for the knapsack and pulling out a towel and a couple of bright blue pieces of material he flung them towards her, saying: 'Go and find somewhere to change. By the time you get back, your lunch should be settled enough for you to go in for a swim.'

Cindy scrambled to her feet and gathered up the towel and bathing suit, only too thankful to escape from the strain of Stuart's company, even if it was only for a little while.

Behind the great black bark further up the beach, Cindy peeled off her sleeveless polo neck top, slacks and underclothing and shook out the bathing suit which she presumed was Delia's, and eyed it in dismay. It might have suited Delia's personality and temperament, but these two bright pieces of material would hardly suit hers. Perhaps if she had had a smooth tan she wouldn't have felt so bad but as it was the colour of the material contrasted noticeably with the white of her skin.

Almost wishing she was dead, or could at least sink through a hole in the sand, she swiftly put on the bikini and wrapped the towel around her so that she was no longer able to feel the sun on her skin. She then proceeded slowly to where she had left Stuart sitting, smoking a cigarette, only to find that he was nowhere to be seen.

Relieved, Cindy dropped the great beach towel to the sand and ran quickly to the shore's edge, then pausing only to hold her breath, she rushed bravely into the waves, gasping and spluttering as their cold arms splashed over and about her.

When she was sure that she was far enough out so that the water came almost to her shoulders, she turned and looked behind her. She waved to Stuart who was standing on the beach in his swimming shorts.

It didn't take him long to swim out to her, his powerful arms cutting through the water and glistening brown in the sun.

'Cold?' he asked her.

With her teeth chattering, she shook her head and immediately experienced a rush of gladness when his lips twitched in amusement. 'Then what are you shivering for?'

'Well, it's not a cold cold, if you know what I mean,' she explained chatteringly. 'It's a bracing cold and so invigorating that it leaves you quite warm.'

He sent her a mocking pitying glance and before turning to swim away, he said: 'Keep moving about and you won't get cold.'

After about twenty minutes, Cindy heard him yell at her: 'Come on, you'd better get out now.'

Cindy, however, was just beginning to forget her brief clothing being some distance away from Stuart and was enjoying herself, letting herself be flung in towards the shore by every breaker. Immediately she made to protest. 'But. . . .'

'But nothing! I'm going in now and I'm not leaving you in by yourself. Get out!' he ordered, then swam strongly to the shore.

Cindy muttered angrily to herself as she flounced out of the surf, battling angrily with the receding tide.

'Don't look so furious,' Stuart drawled lazily, lying back on the warm sand. 'And don't scowl like that. You'll get a furrowed brow, crows feet and pinched mouth and God knows what else. Lie down in the sun.' Already he had closed his eyes and so, not feeling up to defying him, Cindy spread out on her towel and lying back she closed her eyes against the sun.

She didn't know how long she lay there before she realized that a shadow had passed over the sun. 'Odd,' she thought, for there hadn't been a cloud in the sky earlier.

Opening her eyes, she found Stuart leaning on one elbow looking down at her. Her heart leapt with fright. He must have been looking at her for some time, she thought. Suddenly she was aware once more of the briefness of her attire and felt a scorching flush spread over her body followed by a cold one.

She saw his eyes move slowly up over her bare neck and shoulders resting momentarily on the pulse quivering at the base of her throat, then to her mouth and eyes. She felt the coolness of his skin resting against her ribs and thigh as he loomed over her, his wide shoulders immense and frightening.

And his eyes, moody and purposeful. But purposeful in what? Was he still endeavouring to prove himself right? Whatever it was, Cindy gained the impression that he would have acted the same to any girl because he wanted to, not because she was Cindy

Taylor and he wanted to kiss only Cindy Taylor. With something like a sob, she rolled away from him, on to her stomach.

He moved beside her and drew closer to her. He bent and kissed the nape of her neck where the two curtains of dark hair parted, his fingers moving along her spine. 'You're so beautiful. Your skin is so white,' he murmured against her skin.

'There's no emotion in his voice. No thickness in his tones. Nothing!' Cindy realized bleakly. 'He's done this so many times that it just comes natural, no emotion, no feelings, nothing worthwhile.' Even his breath on her skin hadn't quickened.

'Cindy. . . .'

'No!' She twisted free of his hands and sat up, tears pricking her eyelids. 'No, never! You don't care, do you? You don't care about me or for me. I told you once that I wouldn't be just another of your conquests and I won't. Ever!' She paused a moment and then plunged on: 'Your mother was right. You could never love anyone. Not even yourself.'

His mouth tightened. 'What the hell is there to love? In any one person — or myself?'

'There's plenty, Stuart.' She knelt up and sat back on her heels. 'It's just that you haven't met the right people. But you've got to look for them and keep looking. I know you got off to a bad start in more ways than one. When you do find love, though, true love, it'll never desert you. There's a lot of love in you, Stuart, but you try desperately hard to hide it, make out it's not there, that it doesn't exist and not everyone can see through that hard, impenetrable barrier which keeps the good in the inside. . . .'

'But you, oh wise and knowledgeable one, can see through it?'

She nodded. She leaned forward and placed her hands on either side of his face, feeling the rough skin against her palms, and laid her lips gently on his. He stiffened, but he made no move whatsoever to either draw away or bring her closer. She knelt back. 'Please believe me.'

'Okay, Angel. I'll let myself believe that illusion for a little while — just to please you.' He gave a half smile.

Allowing herself to be held by his compelling gaze for a few moments longer, she reluctantly got to her feet. Gathering up her towel, she wrapped it around her shoulders and walked off along the beach towards the black bark, her happiness nearly brimming over.

Stuart waited until she emerged from behind the bark fully dressed once more and started up the beach to him, before he gathered together their odds and ends.

Flinging a towel around his neck, he held out his free hand to her which she clasped warmly and eagerly in hers, sending an unusual warmth through him. He smiled down at her and watched her smile back before lowering her lashes to concentrate on picking her way over the rocks leading up on to the grass.

'Do you mind if we dine out tonight?' Stuart asked that evening after he had spent some time with his mother who had not ventured from her room at all during the remainder of that day. 'Mother has gone out.'

'I see.' Bewildered and feeling rather despondent, Cindy showered and dressed carefully and without hurrying. She combed her freshly washed hair out of its set and left it to bounce heavily on to her shoulders. Slipping on her grey-blue coat over a straight sheath of rich teal guipure lace, she went out to the living-room to where Stuart was waiting for her.

He pressed out the butt of his cigarette and pulled himself up from his lounging position in a deep comfortable chair. In his dark suit and white shirt, he appeared even darker and bigger, at once making her feel feminine and smaller than her five foot eight.

'Ready?'

'Uh huh.'

'And what is that supposed to mean?' he asked, amused.

'Yes — dopey.'

He took her arm and slanted her a sideways glance, his mouth lifting in a half crooked smile.

'He's irresistible,' she thought, looking away from him. 'I can understand now why Jo and the others found him so.'

All his movements were deft and deliberate. Cindy found herself watching for them. The way he opened the car door and slammed it shut, the way he inserted the car key and then turning it, changing gear and twisting the wheel, all in one fluid movement. There was nothing fussy, clumsy or hesitant about his movements. He knew what he was doing, how to do it and he did it.

He didn't ask her whether she had any special preference as to where they dined. Instead he drove at his usual fast pace in the direction of the city. However, Cindy soon realized where they were heading.

'In this your favourite haven?' she asked as he drew to a stop outside the Nicoberg Restaurant.

'Why? Do you still dislike it? It's romantic and has atmosphere.' Stuart turned to grin at her.

Cindy remembered the candlelit table they had sat at when he had taken her to this very same restaurant against her will. 'Yes, I guess it has, but the last time I dined here I wasn't really in a romantic mood.'

'And are you in a romantic mood tonight?' he asked against her ear as he helped her from the car.

'That we'll have to see,' she laughed lightly. 'Doesn't it have something to do with the atmosphere?'

The corner of his lips lifted. He slipped his arm around her to lay it lightly against her back. This

144

time she didn't bring her hand up to dig her nails into the flesh of his.

The same waiter greeted Stuart by name and although the restaurant appeared very crowded, the waiter promised to get him the same table that they had sat at the time before.

Cindy placed her handbag on the side of the table and slipped her coat from her shoulders. She sat down and leaned forward, her arms resting on the table, and looked around her.

It fascinated her to see the way the warm, smoky air swirled beneath dull coloured lights and around the flames on the candles on every table. Then her eyes came back to Stuart. She saw his gaze flicker over her bare arms and neck, their whiteness emphasized by the teal of her frock.

'You look even lovelier through candlelit smoke,' he told her softly.

Cindy tried her best to ignore the exalted beat of her heart. 'You must be feeling romantic tonight. Who was it that said that New Zealand men didn't have a romantic vein in the whole of the male population put together, for they had no need to practise being romantic since the scenery was there to do it all for them?'

'Never mind who it was. Do you believe it?' Watching her behind half closed lids.

'Whoever it was was generalizing, I think, but nevertheless there are numerous cases. New Zealand men like to think they're manly and masculine and hate and scoff at any sign of weakness or softness displayed by another male and many think that by displaying the more romantic emotions or vulnerable side of their nature, they're weak and sappy. They try so hard to prove that they're a man's man, they forget how to treat a girl — romance-wise, that is.'

'I see, oh, knowledgeable and experienced one.'

'You see what? You're laughing at me!'

'Not at all. I see that I'll have to correct that last impression.'

'Oh, you needn't bother. Where you're concerned, I admit I was generalizing by that last remark.' She laughed and looked up to smile at the waiter as he set down their food in front of them.

Later, when their empty plates had been taken away, Stuart lifted his wine glass. Their glasses clinked and he reached over and took her hand in his and entwining his fingers with hers, he murmured, 'Would you like to dance?' Lifting her hand he stood up and led her on to the already crowded dance floor.

Holding her close, Stuart protected her from the other swaying couples whose elbows and shoulders were inclined to knock into her, making her want to creep closer into the circle of his protecting arms. But she didn't have to take the initiative. As the lights dimmed and the music softened, he moved her closer and bent his head so that his rough cheek was resting against her temple.

His jaw suddenly tightened and he lifted his head. Looking down at her he saw the up-sweep of her lashes as she looked at him. Her blue eyes held a misty sparkle as they met his through the smoky air. Then something showed in his eyes. Cindy's smile faded and she strained away from him.

He laughed softly and tightened his hold on her. 'Scaredy cat,' he whispered.

'I'm not!'

'Oh yes, you are. Why do you always shy away from me?'

'Because when you look at me like that you remind me of a — a hungry wolf.'

'Perhaps I am hungry — hungry for love — for your love.'

Cindy closed her eyes. Forcing her voice to remain steady, she snapped: 'You don't mean that, so don't joke about it!'

He merely laughed again. 'Cindy Taylor in love. I can picture you now in love with your Prince Charming, someone quiet and safe like Jo's Keith. Your face radiant and Prince Charming unable to believe what a lucky guy he is. . . . Hey, what's this — you're crying! Well, of all the nutty dames I've met, you take the cake. Honey, what are you crying for?'

'Oh, you dope! Please take me out of here. Everyone will wonder what the matter is. And my mascara will run.'

'The clod I am they'll probably think I've trodden all over your feet,' he said almost tenderly. Taking her arm he led her off the floor.

'Now, tell me what made you cry. Nothing I said that I can remember,' Stuart said when they were once more heading back to Muriwai Beach.

'You made me cry!' It was out before she could stop it. With an exasperated sigh, she continued: 'How can you joke about such things and how do you know that I'm so easily satisfied with someone who is kind, safe and reliable etcetera? I wish you'd stop acting so cynical at my expense. You know nothing about the desires of my heart nor have you ever bothered to find out.'

'Then tell me now.'

The mocking laughter in his voice infuriated her. 'As you are so obviously not sincerely interested, I wouldn't like to risk boring you!' she snapped. 'But in future, would you please refrain from remarking on my personal feelings for you know nothing whatsoever about them, and nor are you likely to.'

Now she had done it. Let her impulsive tongue and temper run away with her. Now they were probably enemies once more.

They sped along in silence — a tense silence which lasted up until they reached his mother's home.

'You know what I think?' Stuart said slowly as he stopped at the top of the driveway. Getting out he came around to open her door. 'I think that you don't know yourself what your true feelings are.'

'Do you just?' Cindy made to walk on ahead of him but was stopped as Stuart's hand descended on her shoulder and swung her around. His hand slipped inside the collar of her coat and rested against the skin of her neck and shoulder, his fingers hard on the back of her neck.

She stiffened and tried to pull back, but his hand refused to allow her to retreat, instead he drew her closer.

'Do you want me to let you go?' he whispered, placing his free hand on the other side of her neck.

She nodded, incapable of any movement or form of speech, feeling as though her whole body had turned to liquid under his hands. Then his mouth was moving along her cheek to rest searchingly on hers. She closed her eyes tightly. She put up her hands to drag his away, but only to find they had a will of their own as they closed on his wrists.

'Still want me to let you go?' Stuart whispered.

'Yes — yes,' she made herself answer, but fully conscious of her hands tightening on his wrists.

'Liar!' he laughed softly, triumphantly. 'Angels shouldn't lie.'

Cindy was fully aware of his gloating victory but for once refused to let herself be ruled by her head. Instead her arms slid up and closed about his neck and her eyes closed against hot tears as he kissed the side of her neck and hollows of her shoulders.

It was no good. It just wasn't any good. She loved him and by refusing to admit it wasn't going to alter the fact just as admitting it wasn't going to do her any good anyway. Oh God, what was going to happen to her now? What was she going to do?

'Now do you know what your feelings are? Are they still mixed up or have I just added to your confusion?' He looked down at her, the expression in his eyes invisible in the darkness, but the line of his mouth was still as hard as ever and slightly amused.

'If either of us is emotionally confused and have need to examine their inner feelings, then I think it is you, Stuart. Sleep on it!' she told him, forcing flippancy into her tones. 'Good night!' She turned and walked away from him in the direction of the bungalow.

CHAPTER SEVEN

THE NEXT morning, Cindy went along to the kitchen for breakfast only to find Kiri Newman there alone, dressed in her dressing gown and pyjamas. Her hair looked as though it had been left uncombed for weeks and her skin was blotchy and puffy around her eyes. Between her slack fingers she held a half smoked cigarette.

Had she been looking her normal self, Cindy still wouldn't have said that Stuart resembled his mother in any way. She felt an overwhelming pity for the woman, who looked pathetic and unhappy. The movement of her hand reaching up to brush back her untidy hair was a gesture of resignation and defeat.

'Would you like me to cook some breakfast? It doesn't look as though you've eaten,' she ventured, glancing around for any sign of soiled dishes and finding none.

'No, thanks. I-I'm not hungry.' Her hands shook as she lifted the cigarette to her taut lips.

'Oh, I see.' Cindy rubbed a knuckle against the tip of her nose. 'Where is Stuart?' she asked after a while. 'Isn't he up yet?'

'Oh yes, he's up all right. Didn't you hear us?'

'Hear what?'

'Oh, just another plurry row. He's walked out. Gone off somewhere.' Kiri's shoulders shook slightly. 'I think that he doesn't want to stay in the house with me.'

'Oh no! You mustn't think that.' Cindy crossed to her side.

Kiri's shoulders hunched as she laid her head on her arms. 'Oh God, what can I do? I know I did wrong in depriving him of a father — but must it go on? Must I go on paying for it for the rest of my life? I don't know how much more I can stand. I love him so much.'

Cindy looked at her helplessly, seeing her misery and knowing there was nothing she could do. 'But if you told him how much you loved him, surely he'd forgive and forget,' she suggested after a while.

Kiri shook her head on her arms. 'No, it's too late now. We never did understand each other. He was always so — so wild and reckless that I didn't know how to handle him and without a man's guidance, which was what he needed, I was hopelessly out of my depth, and there I made my second mistake. I gave up. There was absolutely no communication between us. He went his way and I went mine, neither of us needing the other, or rather not realizing just how great our need was — until now and now it's too late.

'He hates me more now than before because of Delia . . .'

'Delia?'

Kiri nodded. 'I let him down and he thought that was bad enough. Never did he think that two women could be so much alike. She let him down too and now I think he loathes all women. But me especially because being a mother I, at least, should have been above all that — someone he could look up to.

'He's grown so hard and ruthless, he frightens me at times and I don't know what to do. What can I do?' She was obviously working herself up into an overwrought state of nerves.

Gently, Cindy lifted her thin shoulders and murmuring to her coaxingly, she managed to persuade her to let her put her back to bed.

When at last Kiri was resting peacefully, Cindy left the house to search for Stuart and found him strolling along the sea's edge, his hands in the pockets of his blue jeans and his head bent.

She ran down to him, her feet making no sound on the sand. 'Stuart.' She put her hand up to touch his arm.

He started visibly and turned on her, his expression withdrawn, cold and somehow frightening. 'What do you want?' he scowled.

Obviously seeing her brought no reminder to him of what had happened between them the night before. She knew that it had been merely a passing episode to him, but nevertheless, she couldn't suppress the sharp thrust of disappointment rising in her throat.

Determinedly, she pushed all thought of herself out of her mind and thought only of the wretched woman lying on her bed up in the bungalow. 'Don't speak to me like that!' she snapped back at him, all at once very angry. 'I've just put your mother to bed.'

'Why did you need to do that? She's quite capable of putting herself to bed.' His lips curled scathingly.

Cindy looked at him disbelievingly. 'You really are a fink, aren't you?' she said. 'You make me sick! Your mother is nearly out of her mind about you.'

'My mother is a good actress.'

'Your mother loves you — can't you see that? She knows she's done you out of a father and she's sorry — really she is — and she loves you.'

'Kiri Newman has loved no one in her life other than Kiri Newman. If this wasn't true then she wouldn't have left my father.'

'You're her son, Stuart. Don't tell me that you feel nothing for her?'

Stuart remained silent.

'Stuart,' she prodded. 'Forgive and forget what's happened in the past. You're so filled up with vengeance and self-pity that you can't see straight. You're ruining yourself and her. Please, Stuart, make it up with her now, you may not get another chance.'

But there was no budging Stuart. They left later that afternoon, and still he hadn't done as she had asked.

Perhaps he didn't love her as Cindy had felt sure he did, despite his outward display of contempt for her. She sat next to him in the car feeling utterly helpless.

She herself loved him and wanted to help him but she knew the bitter frustration of realizing that she just didn't have the power to reach him and probably never would. She could understand very well the private hell that his mother must be going through and must have experienced for many years. 'Is the same going to happen to me?' Cindy wondered.

Monday dawned dark and bleak with thick, low clouds hovering threateningly over the city and also over most of the country. An abrupt and unwelcome change after the week-end weather.

The forecast stated that most of New Zealand was to expect violent electrical storms and gale force winds as the result of a huge hurricane which was approaching swiftly towards the northern tip of the South Island and the lower part of the North Island. As soon as it hit the country it wouldn't be very long before it reached the Northern Districts.

Stuart rang and told Cindy to take the day off for if the storm should hit Auckland as violently as it was feared to do, then it could be dangerous to venture out into the thick of it, especially coming back and forth to work.

However, the storm didn't break until later that night and it seemed to have gained strength from its long wait. Cindy lay in bed, unable to sleep as the storm raged on, and watched as the lightning illuminated her room. She listened to the thunder, the lashing winds and the torrents of heavily falling rain.

By the time morning came the storm had quietened and had almost blown itself out, leaving behind trails of damage in its wake throughout most of the North Island.

Auckland had been the worst hit by far. Uprooted trees and power poles. Cars had been upturned by the wind and many people injured as a result, iron roofs had been lifted off houses which were situated on the more elevated and less sheltered areas and had been strewn across the roads.

Cindy left for work in the pouring rain. She accepted Keith's offer to drive her into town, and sat in silence, her mood as glum as the weather, as she witnessed what rather heart breaking damage the hurricane had caused.

To escape from getting wetter than was absolutely necessary, she ducked through the front entrance of the hotel and into the foyer, instead of going around to the staff entrance.

She saw Sue at the reception desk, talking to someone on the phone. She was just about to pass the desk when Sue raised a hand to motion her to stop.

Cindy waited until she had hung up and then asked, eyeing the girl's worried face: 'What is it, Sue? You look a bit put out. Nothing wrong, is there?'

Sue nodded. 'I'm afraid so. Mr. Newman rang to say he won't be in today. His mother — she was killed last night. She was outside when the storm hit — she must have dashed out for something — and was hit by a bit of flying débris. She — was killed instantly.'

Cindy's hand flew to her mouth, her eyes widening in horror. 'Oh no!'

'He rang Bob just a while ago. He said he sounded very strange, shock probably.'

'Poor Stuart, how terrible, after he had just spent the week-end with her too. When did he find out, do you know?'

'Apparently he rang to make sure that she was all right sometime last night, but he got no answer so he drove out to Muriwai Beach only to find her already dead.'

'Is he still out there?'

'As far as I know.'

Cindy gripped the edge of the desk. 'Perhaps I should go out to him.'

'No. Bob said that he wanted you to cancel any appointments he may have and to go on with the work he set out for you yesterday. He said he'd be in later this afternoon.'

Cindy nodded and went on up to her office. She couldn't concentrate on her work and found herself making the silliest of mistakes, her mind too full of Stuart alone in the storm battered bungalow at Muriwai Beach where he had found his mother lying dead.

The afternoon dragged unbearably. She had heard no word from Stuart and by the time five-thirty arrived, he had still not arrived back at the office.

Finally, Cindy couldn't stand it any longer. She was going to his home. Perhaps he had returned and had gone straight home. She struggled into her rain coat and tied her cherry red scarf over her hair. Pulling on her boots and gathering up her handbag she ran down to where she found Sue on duty at the reception desk.

'Sue! You're still here?'

'I've just come on. I knocked off shortly after ten this morning.'

'Still no word?'

Sue shook her head.

'Look Sue, I've got an awful feeling something's wrong. Can I borrow your car — please? I promise I'll be careful.'

'Of course. But I didn't know you could drive.'

'I've been driving tractors and Dad's jeep all over

the farm since I was a kid, but I haven't a licence. Please, Sue, I'll go carefully.'

Sue eyed her doubtfully, but nevertheless handed her the keys. 'Okay, but it's your funeral. Make sure you do go carefully — those roads are like glass.'

'Thanks, Sue.' Cindy grabbed the keys from her and ran out of the hotel to where Sue parked her shiny red Hillman Imp in the staff parking lot.

She took no chances but drove carefully and steadily out towards Stuart's home. Pulling up outside the front door, she got out and was thankful to see light coming from one of the side windows. However, it wasn't Stuart who answered the door, but instead his housekeeper, Elizabeth Reefton.

'Oh, Mrs. Reefton, I'm Mr. Newman's secretary, is he in — do you think I could see him?' Cindy asked breathlessly.

'I'm afraid Mr. Newman isn't at home at the moment, Miss . . .'

'Taylor, Cindy Taylor.'

'Of course, the young girl he brought home one night, soaking wet. Come in.'

'Thank you.' Cindy stepped into the hall and followed the woman through into the lounge.

'Sit down, near the fire, I'll make you some coffee.'

Cindy opened her mouth to protest, but Elizabeth had already left the lounge. Nervously, and on edge, she sat down and waited impatiently for her to return.

'Where is Stuart?' Cindy stood up as Elizabeth came back with the coffee.

'Stuart is still over at Muriwai Beach.'

'But he's been there all day!'

'And most of last night.'

'I heard about his mother. I'm sorry about that.'

'Don't waste your sympathies on Stuart. He has plenty for himself. He's probably wallowing in self-pity right now and probably has been for the past eighteen hours.'

Cindy looked at her in surprise. 'Isn't that rather heartless?'

'But true. Where are you going?' Elizabeth looked up as Cindy got to her feet once more.

'To Muriwai Beach, to find him. He may need some help.'

Elizabeth Reefton laughed. 'You'll probably get abused left, right and centre. I wouldn't advise anyone to try and talk to him right now, and certainly not someone like you.'

'Nevertheless I'm going.'

Elizabeth was silent for a minute as she studied the young girl confronting her. 'Are you in love with him?'

Cindy tilted her head defiantly, but didn't reply.

'I thought it might happen, as soon as I saw the attraction he held for you after only a brief meeting. But for your sake I prayed that it wouldn't. Does he know?'

'Know what?'

Elizabeth smiled sadly and patted the space on the sofa beside her. 'Sit down, Cindy.'

Cindy sensed the seriousness in the woman's manner, and felt that what she was about to say would be of benefit to her, so slowly, she did as she was told.

'Has he ever told you about his mother — or Delia?'

Cindy shook her head.

'Then perhaps it is only fair that you should know, in these circumstances, that is. How old are you, Cindy?'

'Twenty.'

Elizabeth nodded. 'Yes, you're very young. Delia Lawrence was twenty-five, a very experienced twenty-five. Believe me she had lived those years to the hilt. There had been other men before Stuart, just as there had been other women before her in Stuart's life. But Stuart had never fallen in love. He vowed that he never would because of the way his mother had let him and his father down, but then he met Delia and he fell like a ton of bricks. She was beautiful, vivacious and popular with all members of the opposite sex.

'Stuart knew full well what type of woman she was, but he still loved her and wanted to marry her and although she professed to love him, she didn't want any part of marriage. Life for her was still too exciting and eventful, so she tried everything to make him let her stay here and live with him as his wife. However, because he loved her and wanted to marry her, he wouldn't allow this. Many a time she would leave here, furious because she had lost another heated row with Stuart. He was in love with her and just as passionate and possessive as any man in his position. But the mistake he made was when he put her on a pedestal she didn't deserve; giving her far more respect than was her due.

'At last, when she found that he was not to be budged from his decision, she walked out on him. On the eve of their wedding, calling him everything. That he was merely an apology for a man and that if she married it would be to a man, not a mouse. Then, as if to spite him, she up and married some rich Australian business tycoon who was staying at the hotel. Now, as far as I know, she's living in Aussie. So you can see why he is bitter towards women.

'He told me that never again would he respect any female. "They're not worth it," he told me, "and they don't want it, so from now on I'm going to treat them exactly the way they want to be treated." '

Cindy murmured after a lengthy pause: 'What a fool she was. He would never love me like that. What about his mother?'

'Kiri Newman was married during the war. She wed an American soldier who was stationed at Paraparumu, and so, naturally, went to live in the States. She was very much in love at the time, but after many years she got homesick for New Zealand and wanted to come back. Unfortunately, her husband wouldn't leave America so Kiri stuck it out over there for about twelve years.

'By this time, Stuart was fourteen, and an only child, so Kiri left her husband and brought Stuart back to New Zealand with her, to the country where he was born.

'He didn't want to come here, so to make him agree to come, Kiri promised to let him go back after a few months. Of course he never did go back. Kiri didn't have the money and whatever money her husband sent over from the States, she used to get herself started up in a small, profitable business for herself and Stuart.

'Stuart wrote to his father regularly and he had made up his mind to go back to the States when his schooling was through — but his father died when Stuart reached the age of eighteen.

'It was tragic to see the change in him. The way he treated his mother whom he never did forgive for the way in which she had tricked him. And it was also tragic to see the change in Kiri.

'Then when Stuart was successful in his own right at the age of twenty-seven, with the help of the money left to him by his father, he put her up in that peaceful little bungalow at Muriwai Beach, with a housekeeper and someone to do the gardens several times a week. She thought that he had forgiven her. Only when he failed to visit her for weeks, sometimes months, at a time did she realize that she had been nursing a rather hopeless dream.'

'I see.' Cindy looked down at her empty mug and scratched her nail over its pattern which looked as though it had merely been painted on. 'Thank you for telling me all this. Now perhaps I can understand things a little better.'

'Are you still going out to him then?' Elizabeth asked as Cindy got up and placed her mug on the coffee table.

Cindy nodded.

'Well,' Elizabeth sighed, 'I can't stop you from going if you feel you must go. You may love him and feel sorry for him, but don't do anything you'll regret. He'll probably scoff and hurl sarcasm at you, but ignore it. It shows he doesn't really believe that you're another Delia, so don't destroy his belief, for it could do more harm to him than it would to you.'

Cindy nodded again and tied her scarf over her hair. She followed Elizabeth into the hall and turned to face her as she opened the door. 'Thank you again for what you've told me, and for your advice. Of course I wouldn't do anything to hurt him. I love him too much for that.'

Elizabeth smiled. 'I really believe you do, and I know he wouldn't be a very easy man to love. You must have plenty of courage to have stood by him the way you have. Let's hope he comes to his senses before it's too late and he loses you.'

'Oh, he'll never lose me. I think that's where courage comes into it. If he does throw me over, I'll need all the courage I can get. Well, good-bye.'

Elizabeth gripped the young girl's hand warmly and watched as the rear lights of the Hillman Imp disappeared down the long curving drive.

For the first time since she had known Stuart, she felt the apprehension and worry she harboured for him slip away, and something warm take its place. It looked as though life might take a turn for the better for perhaps the first time in Stuart's life. And it would, if Cindy Taylor had anything to do about it. What a blessing in disguise a rainy night and a muddy puddle could turn out to be.

There were no lights shining from the windows of the bungalow when Cindy arrived. In fact everything was so dark and quiet, except for the rough roaring of the sea, it struck her as being eerie and rather frightening.

She felt her way carefully along the rain-flooded path leading up to the steps of the patio. She was thankful to find the double glass doors opening into the lounge were not locked and so stepping into the dark interior, she ran her hand over the wall. Finding the light switch, she flicked it on, but nothing happened. Dismayed, she suddenly realized that somewhere along the road the power lines must have been torn down.

She found her way out into the passage and tried calling Stuart's name, and even though her voice was barely above a whisper, she managed to scare herself. She stopped outside the bedroom Stuart had occupied during the week-end. She groped forward and put her hand out to touch the bed and immediately felt the hardness of Stuart's shoulder. She found that he was lying on his stomach and by running her hand over his back, she discovered that his shirt was damp and icy with perspiration.

'Stuart!' she said urgently, giving his shoulder a shake. 'Stuart!' But he never uttered a sound nor moved a muscle.

'Blast it all, if only there was some light!' She slipped her hand inside his trouser pockets for his lighter and his car keys, suddenly remembering that he had a miniature torch attached to the leather key case.

It was astonishing just how much light was afforded by the tiny thing, but there still wasn't enough to discover what kind of state Stuart was in, or find out how she could help him.

After searching around in the cupboards in the kitchen, she found an old but serviceable kerosene lamp. She gave it a gentle shake and listened carefully for the splash that would tell her whether it had enough kerosene in it to be lit. She set the flame of Stuart's lighter to the wick and breathed a silent prayer as its glow lit up the kitchen, just as well as any electric light would have done.

Back in the bedroom, she placed the lamp on the bedside table and looked down at Stuart lying flat out on his front with one arm dangling over the side of the bed. It seemed that he was almost in a coma. His head was turned sideways on the pillow and his hair was ruffled and damp.

She shook him again, but he just remained limp under her hands. She tried to turn him over, but his motionless form was like a dead weight.

Leaving him, Cindy fetched a bowl from the kitchen and filled it with warm water and took it back to the bedroom, collecting a flannel and towel as she went. She was relieved to find that Stuart had turned over on to his back of his own accord. His shirt was unbuttoned down the front, leaving bare his dark torso and chest.

She finished bathing his face and neck and then tried to remove his wet shirt, but paused as he moved suddenly. His head twisted from side to side on the pillow and then became still when he was facing away from the lamp.

'Turn the light off!' she heard him mutter and quickly leaned over to turn the flame down lower.

'How — how are you feeling, Stuart?' she asked idiotically.

'How the hell do you think I'm feeling!' he retorted thickly. 'What are you doing here anyway? Can't a guy have a bit of privacy without having some goddamned, interfering female hanging around?'

'I thought you might need help, and you do.'

'I can help myself!'

'Don't talk such stupid rot, and take that shirt off! You've got pneumonia or something!'

'I've never been sick in my life.' He pushed her hands away. 'Go on! Scram!' He rolled over.

'Stop being so self-pitying and get that shirt off!'

He turned on to his back once more, and looked up at her. 'Look baby, if you don't clear off in a minute, then you're not going to get another chance.'

Cindy stiffened and sat up away from him. 'I'm only trying to help.'

'Look, will you get outta here! I don't care what you're trying to do!'

She hesitated a few seconds and then quickly leapt to her feet as he heaved himself off the bed and swayed unsteadily on his feet.

'God!' he breathed and shut his eyes against the searing pain in his head. He put out a hand to grab something that would support him, but his hand found nothing but thin air.

In a flash, Cindy reached him and in an effort to support him, she put both of her hands under his armpits. She felt his weight as he leaned on her and the heaviness of his head against her neck.

'She's dead.' She heard his muffled tones.

'I — I know.'

'Why did she have to die?'

'Perhaps you didn't love her enough,' she said, and immediately wished she hadn't. She felt his whole body shudder under her hands and felt his shoulders rack and knew that he was crying. She had never seen a man cry before, and never did she ever suspect that Stuart was even capable of tears. This probably was the first time he had ever cried, in a great many years.

It shocked Cindy to see this big arrogant man humbling himself to such an extent, but at the same time it filled her with a sad kind of gladness at discovering that she had suspected right. He wasn't without love for his mother, and perhaps loved her more than anyone ever knew. But because he was unsure of himself and of his mother, he kept his love for her hidden behind that barrier he had built around his feelings and emotions. Both mother and son had too much pride to form a relationship they had both wanted so much.

Because Stuart's weight was becoming too heavy for her to support, she sat down with him on the edge of the bed.

Quieter and feeling heavy with sleep, Stuart closed his eyes, his head dropping forward on to her shoulder. Suddenly his sleepiness left him as he became aware of the fragrance of her skin and hair, the softness of her shoulder under his cheek.

'Stay with me.'

Cindy closed her eyes tightly. She realized his need of her to help him push all thought of his mother from his mind, but she couldn't and wouldn't bring herself to fulfil that need.

Gently, she pushed him away and stood up, her back facing him. 'I can't.'

Stuart forced a laugh. 'Still God's human angel — right to the end, eh?'

She saw him lumber past her towards the door.

'Where are you going?' she asked anxiously.

'I need some air. Heaven's swirling, white mists don't altogether agree with me — the state I'm in.'

Cindy ran after him. 'But it's raining out there.'

'Just what I need.'

'Please, Stuart! Don't be a fool. You'll get pneumonia for sure dressed like that in the pouring rain!' She tried to take hold of his arm as he stumbled down the patio steps and out on to the lawn, but with an impatient hand he managed to shake her off.

'Please, Stuart . . .' She ran by his side, feeling the grass squelch under her feet.

'Oh, for God's sake quit whining at me and get out of here!' he snarled, turning on her.

She stopped, aware of the change in him, a change which frightened the life out of her.

'Go on, get!' His hand descended on one shoulder with bone-cracking pressure and, turning her around, he pushed her away from him towards the drive.

She hit the ground with such force that for a moment she could only lie there, dazed with shock and pain which raged through her shoulder as it came in contact with a piece of jutting rock at the side of the drive.

By the time she had struggled to her feet, Stuart had disappeared into the darkness. It was useless trying to go after him, but she would have to get help. He was heading in the direction of the sea, and in his present state he could be capable of anything. Even if nothing happened to him he could pass out anywhere along the beach and by the time he came to he could be seriously ill.

CHAPTER EIGHT

'PAUL,' Cindy thought, 'I'll have to get hold of him somehow. Stuart said he had an apartment in Karangahape Road. I'll look in the phone book and see if he's listed.'

By the time Cindy had found Paul's apartment, she was feeling almost ready to pass out herself. Her shoulder was aching unbearably so that, and the lack of food and sufficient sleep the night before, gave her the illusion that everything around her was revolving around, slowly and dizzily.

'Cindy Taylor!' Paul exclaimed. 'Good grief, what on earth's the matter with you? You look as white as a sheet. Come on in.'

Vaguely, Cindy was aware that he hadn't yet got ready for bed. She followed him inside and let him take off her coat and drenched scarf.

'I'll make you some coffee and then you can tell me about it.'

'No — no, please,' Cindy protested, closing her eyes against the dizzy spinning of the room.

'Here, you'd better sit down.'

'No, I can't. It's Stuart.' She pushed his hands away from her arms.

'Stuart?' His tone sharpened.

'Yes, out at his mother's bungalow. He's roaming around outside, he's ill. I — I left him wandering off in the direction of the sea. I couldn't make him go back inside . . .'

'Damn fool!' Paul muttered to himself. He dashed out of the room and came back a little later with his coat. 'Look, you stay here . . .'

'No, I'm coming with you.'

166

'No, you're not.' He propelled her into another room which was presumably his bedroom. He sat her on the bed and took the boots from her feet and forcing her to lie back, he covered her with a warm blanket. 'Now you stay put.'

'Jo . . .'

'Don't worry about Jo. I'll give her a ring. I'll be back as soon as I can.'

Cindy awoke the next morning to the dull ache in her shoulder. She sat up suddenly, upon discovering her unfamiliar surroundings, and winced as her shoulder throbbed painfully.

Remembering what had taken place the night before, she quickly climbed out of bed and pulled on her damp boots. She smoothed down her crumpled frock and untidy hair and went out into the lounge where she found Paul, fully clothed, lying asleep on the sofa, clasping the corner of a rug which had long ago slipped on to the floor.

'Paul!' She shook his shoulder until he awoke with a start.

He sat up drowsily and swung his feet over the side of the sofa. 'Hell, my neck!' He rubbed his hand over the side of his neck and tentatively turned his head sideways.

'What happened last night?' Cindy asked impatiently.

'Nothing.'

'But you went out to Muriwai Beach?'

'Yeah, yeah. When I got there I found Stuart stretched out asleep in his bedroom. He was wet through but had taken off his shirt and had wrapped himself in a few woollen blankets, so I left him there.'

'Oh, that rotter! He probably frightened me deliberately, just out of spite!' Cindy raged, exasperated and yet relieved.

'That's probably exactly what he did do. That's Stuart!' Paul stood up, running a hand over his neck and unshaven face. He glanced down at his watch. 'It's eight-thirty. What time do you start work?'

'Nine o'clock. Did you ring Jo?'

'Yes. I told her exactly what happened. I hope that's okay by you?'

Cindy nodded. 'I guess so.'

Cindy answered Jo and Keith's questions as briefly as possible and didn't volunteer or enlarge on any of the information Paul had already given them. In the finish they gave up, thinking it better to let it come naturally, for she would tell them when this cloud of depression had lifted and she felt more like herself.

'In the meantime it would be wiser to leave her alone,' Jo thought, however she was still unable to ease her apprehension.

Cindy arrived at work a little later than her normal starting time only to find Stuart would more than likely be absent until after his mother's funeral which was to take place at three that afternoon.

The pain in her shoulder had subsided considerably after her hot bath and thorough massage, but her bleak mood failed to lift at all during the day.

She worked steadily and automatically and wasn't even aware that Stuart had returned to the hotel until Sue came into the office at about five-thirty to tell her that he was wanting to see her. 'He's gone up to his suite with Paul Brent.'

'Thanks, Sue. I'll take the sheets he left me to type. He probably wants to see them.'

Too impatient to wait for the elevator, which seemed to have been held up on the middle floor, Cindy went on in the direction of the stairway.

Among the people descending the stairs, she suddenly caught a glimpse of Paul who, to her, looked rueful and a bit put out. It could have been her imagination of course, but it was obvious that he was too deeply occupied with his own thoughts to see anyone either coming or going on the stairs, so she hurried on past him, up to the top floor.

She found Stuart sitting on the edge of an armchair in the lounge of his suite. His shoulders bowed and his head resting on his hands.

Swiftly, Cindy closed the door and crossed to his side. Crouching down on one knee, she touched his shoulder. 'Stuart — are you hurt?'

He shrank away from her touch as though it burned. He lifted his head and stared down at her upturned face, his own face drawn and his eyes dark and slightly blank. Suddenly he started laughing, mirthlessly, until Cindy, her nerves at screaming point, covered her ears and shouted at him to stop.

He stopped abruptly. 'God — and you almost had me fooled!'

'What — what do you mean? What's wrong?' Cindy asked bewilderedly.

'Get up off your knees for the love of Mike! What was it I called you — a human angel of God? Well, at one time perhaps, but now you're no better than the rest of them. Oh — you make me sick!'

Shocked, Cindy slowly got to her feet.

'Well, don't just stand there — get out! I can't bear the sight of you!'

'I want to know what I'm supposed to have done first.' She spoke in cold tones.

He laughed again. 'Oh, come on . . . O.K., I'll humour you. You are a change from most I'll give you that.' His voice changed then, and became hard and his question was as sharp as a pistol shot. 'Do you deny that when you left me last night, you went around to Paul's apartment?'

'Oh, that!' Cindy almost uttered a laugh of relief. 'Yes — yes, I did.'

Stuart's expression fell immediately, as though he

had half expected her to deny it and prove to him that it had indeed been untrue. Getting to his feet, he crossed to the window, not looking at her and clenching his hands in his pockets.

'But Stuart, it isn't what you think.' Cindy caught at his arm. He shook her hand off but remained silent and listened to her halting explanation of what had happened.

'Do you really expect me to believe that?' Stuart drawled at last.

'But it's true!' Cindy stamped her foot in frustration.

Stuart turned on her. 'I asked you to stay with me last night. Remember? I also remember your answer: "I can't". It never entered my head that you would be leaving me to go to my best friend, Paul Brent, of all people. You kept your secret pretty well. Congratulations. If I had known —

'You and your pious ideals and high moral standards!' he scorned. 'You and your morale-boosting words to me on Muriwai Beach on Saturday. You almost had me believing your childish lectures — and it was all nothing but a farce, put over so easily with the help of two wide eyes and an innocent face!'

Both shocked and hurt, Cindy retaliated: 'How dare you talk like this to me! I don't have to take it from you or anyone. What you're saying is nothing but a pack of lies — you won't believe what you don't want to believe. You'd much rather go on believing that I'm just like Delia because you don't want to admit that you're wrong and that you've always been wrong!'

Her defiance and highly held head made Stuart want to hurt her more, hurt her more than he had been hurt himself. He smiled at her, his manner suddenly calm and even a little bored. 'I admit I was tricked, not so thoroughly by you but by Paul. We had a bet . . .'

'A — a bet!'

'That's right. Paul owns a twelve-point stag head which I have always wanted. He knew this and bet me that if I could make you mine in the inside of a month, then the head was mine.'

'You — you mean to tell me that — that *you* bet with my self-respect, *my life,* for a mere whim — a stag head!'

'Not so much a whim. That stag head was a prize one. If I didn't win then I would have been obliged to go hunting with Paul, so either way I didn't mind whether I won or lost, for we were to stay in the bush until I had hunted down an even twelve-pointer for myself. But it's the thought of him turning dirty on me and getting in before me really gets my goat.'

Stuart watched her with cruel amusement. He saw her go white to the lips and her eyes darkened and stared at him unseeingly. She turned and walked towards the door, but before she could open it, Stuart was there before her, pulling it open.

Her mind closed just as the door behind her closed, with a final sounding click. She couldn't think clearly and wasn't the least bit aware of the activity of the people going on about her. The only part of her functioning at all seemed to be her legs, automatically carrying her down the stairs, across the foyer and out of the hotel. .

She didn't know why she stepped out from the edge of the pavement and on to the road, without first, out of habit, looking both ways; or why her legs immediately ceased functioning when she was dazzled by the glare of oncoming car lights and deafened by the sounds of screeching brakes and a loud, piercing blast from a horn. Then suddenly there was nothing at all. No lights, no sound, no feeling — just welcome oblivion.

CHAPTER NINE

IT WAS some two to three days before Cindy showed any signs of regaining consciousness. However, to those who waited at her bedside, it seemed more like years. At last, when the curtain of blackness lifted from her brain, Cindy opened her eyes to the late evening sun forcing its way through the half-shut venetian blinds and shining over the polished surface of the floor.

By the bareness of the room and the odour of antiseptic, Cindy guessed where she was. She looked around her, puzzled, until her memory slowly began to come back. With a struggle, she tried to sit up but failed and lay back against the pillows and closed her eyes.

She heard the movements of people about her, low voices, the squeak of rubber soles on slippery floors and the swishing of starched uniforms, but knew nothing more until the next morning.

She awoke feeling considerably better, although her spirits remained just about zero. She found herself unable to rise to the nurse's cheerful chatter and answered the doctor's questions briefly and tonelessly.

During the weeks that followed, she was subjected to innumerable X-rays and tests. She was well aware of the lifelessness in her legs and surprised herself at discovering that she wasn't at all afraid or apprehensive. She couldn't move her legs and when the doctor informed her of this, she took the news without blinking an eyelid. She just didn't care.

'As far as we can find in the tests and X-rays there is nothing physically wrong,' Doctor Perawiti explained. 'I can't say how long this will last but I'm sure it's only a temporary paralysis. You'll be receiving physiotherapy treatment every day. It will help the progress which could be frustrating and slow but that will be entirely up to you and how well you co-operate.'

However, as the weeks passed, Cindy's depression grew and her progress was nil. She saw Jo and Keith every evening and also her parents who travelled up to visit her every so often. Even though she was adamant in her refusal to allow Stuart in to see her, he still continued to visit the hospital with some vain hope that she might change her mind.

Finally, Doctor Perawiti began to suspect the reason for her lack of progress and spoke to her about it.

'I just don't want to see him!' Cindy turned away from the doctor. 'I wish you'd tell him to stop coming. I won't change my mind.'

'Now listen to me, Cindy. You have to have a will to get well. If you haven't got that then you might never walk again. I want you to see this guy; for your own sake. To me he seems to be the very person who holds the key to your depression and emotional state.'

'I won't see him! I won't!' Cindy lay rigidly facing the window.

'You're behaving like a spoilt child. Either you see Mr. Newman and settle your differences with him, or I'm going to have to discharge you from the hospital. There's nothing wrong with you that we can cure without your full co-operation. Now what's your answer going to be? Remember you're not only hurting yourself but your family as well, worrying them needlessly. If you won't think of yourself — think of them.'

Doctor Perawiti waited patiently for her answer. He was a quiet, serious kind of man, qualities which were usually unusual in most of the Maoris Cindy knew in Apiti. But he still possessed a great sense of fun and a big kind nature which succeeded, at times, in lifting her depression.

'Okay, I'll see him,' Cindy replied in muffled tones.

'Good girl. I'll send him in when he arrives.'

Cindy remained in her position with her back to the door until the room darkened and night fell. She refused to eat her dinner but waited in the darkness for Stuart to arrive.

As the evening dragged on, she felt the first spasms of emotion since the accident. Her heart would beat rapidly whenever she heard footsteps approaching her room, only to feel it sink with something she refused to acknowledge as disappointment when the footsteps continued past her door.

Perhaps he wasn't coming tonight. Perhaps he had finally decided to give up trying to see her. Perhaps he wouldn't be coming any more. Cindy was surprised to feel fear as these suspicions ran through her mind.

'Cindy?'

She jumped at the sound of Stuart's voice coming from the doorway. She turned her head and saw his big frame outlined beside the door. All at once her fear fled and was replaced by a gladness which made her want to both laugh and cry, to get out of bed, if she could, and rush to him and fling her arms around him, to say she was sorry. But she never did any of these things. Instead she lay quite still and silent.

'Cindy, are you asleep?'

Courage had failed her. Then she saw that by his outline he was turning to go and so forced herself to answer. 'No.' She saw his head lower as he turned back.

He was silent for a moment. 'Do you want the light on?'

'No. There's a chair by the bed.'

She waited tensely while he pulled out the chair and sat down beside the bed. The silence between them seemed almost unbearable.

'How are you feeling?' Stuart asked irrelevantly after a while.

'Fine. There's nothing the matter with me.'

'I know you can't walk.'

'Oh that!' Cindy gave a mirthless laugh. 'Doctor Perawiti informs me that it's all in my mind and that I could walk if I wanted to.'

'And you don't want to?'

'Why should I?' she said bitterly.

Stuart didn't answer. At last he spoke: 'I don't know what to say or how to say it, but I would — I'd rather have been killed myself than have this happen to you. It's my fault and I'm sorry.'

'Why should you be sorry? I'm not. It was an accident, I walked out in front of the car — you didn't push me, so don't feel that it was your fault this has happened.'

'I've seen Paul since your accident.'

'Oh yes? Well, at least you have proof that I haven't crept out of hospital one night in order to spend it at his apartment,' Cindy said sarcastically.

Stuart avoided answering her jibe. 'You know apologizing doesn't come easy to me and because of what I said to you up there in my suite I can't expect you to forgive me. Paul told me the truth soon after the accident. That he was only joking when he told me about you and him, but I had not given him a chance to explain.'

There was a pause during which Cindy clenched at the bed with her hands. Her nails rasped against the coarse linen beneath the blankets.

'I could have cut my tongue out,' Stuart went on, his voice deep with feeling. 'I'm the cause of your accident. If I hadn't got so carried away this would never have happened.'

Cindy remained silent, waiting, hoping, wanting him to go on, to tell her that he believed her and that he was lying about the bet.

'Won't you say something? I can't sleep for thinking that you may not walk again, regardless of the doctor saying that your progress is up to you. If you won't forgive me, won't you have mercy on me? Please co-operate with the doctors and give me back what little peace of mind I once had.'

Cindy closed her eyes, disappointment flooding through her. 'You needn't worry about whether I walk again or not. You needn't lose any sleep over it. The fact that I can't walk doesn't worry me . . .'

'Then what is it?'

'Do you believe — really believe that absolutely nothing happened that night at Paul's apartment?' she asked quietly.

'Yes. I think if I had really thought about it at the time, instead of being, as you had pointed out, so willing to believe ill of any female, I would have seen the truth in what you said.'

'You're not — not just saying that because you hope I'll get well . . .'

'No, honey, I'm not. I believe you and you must believe me.'

'And — and the bet?' she whispered.

'The bet?'

'Yes. The one between you and Paul?'

'That, I'm afraid and ashamed to admit, is true. Paul and I did have a bet but I called it off before we spent the week-end with my mother at Muriwai Beach; that time Paul came to my office.'

'You called it off then? Why?'

'Because I knew you better then than I did when I first met you. You're innocence and fixed ideals got under my skin, but I felt ashamed to think that I was plotting to have you fall for me just for the sake of a bet. With anyone else it wouldn't have worried me, but you were different. Untouched and unspoilt and also because I had made a promise to my house-keeper the first night I took you home.'

'What was that promise?'

'To leave you untouched and unspoilt.'

'Would you have broken that promise if I had wanted you to?'

'Yes,' Stuart said frankly. 'I only gave my promise on the condition that you had to be an unwilling party. That was the main theme of our bet. I had to make you a willing party.'

'I see. Stuart, why did you let me believe that the bet was still on between you and Paul?'

'Because I guess I wanted to hurt you. The thought of you and Paul together maddened me beyond all reason. When I called that bet off that morning Paul came to my office at the hotel, it was because for the first time in my life, I think, I discovered I had such a thing as a conscience.'

'Oh, Stuart!' Cindy gave a choked little laugh, tears of gladness trickling down from the corners of her eyes.

'What is it?' Stuart shifted his position and sat down on the edge of the bed. 'Why are you crying? You're not in pain or anything?'

'No.' She laughed through her tears and impulsively put up her arms and slipping them around his neck she hugged him tight.

He tensed and then, wonderingly, disentangled her arms from around his neck and said: 'What does this mean? That you forgive me for being the cause behind you lying here like this?'

'Lying here like this is the least of my worries, I told you that. Just as long as you really believe me and that what you said — or part of what you said about the bet was untrue, then everything is okay.'

'But I don't understand. Your legs . . .'

'My legs — they'll do as I tell 'em!' she laughed softly. 'I'll walk again you'll see. I'll be walking again before you know where you are. I'm sorry you spent so many sleepless nights on my account but I didn't refuse to walk deliberately. I just lost all will to want to walk again.'

She felt his hand move to the side of her face. 'Stuart, please turn on the light.'

'No. You don't know what a sight a man looks when he has spent many sleepless nights.'

'Why, Stuart! I do believe you're vain!' Cindy teased, her fingers exploring the nape of his neck and the line of his jaw.

'I am not!' he retorted swiftly, drawing back.

'A typical New Zealand male, eh?' she laughed. 'Refuses to admit he has any weaknesses that may detract from his masculinity.'

'Puss-cat!' she heard him murmur under his breath as he got to his feet.

'Will you come and see me tomorrow?' she pleaded.

'Sure, honey.'

'When you've had a good night's sleep — you'll look better then,' she couldn't resist adding and with a scream she pulled the blankets up over her head as he advanced menacingly towards the bed.

After he had gone, Cindy lay in the darkness, wide awake and happy. A smile curved her mouth for the first time in a long while. She would walk again — and soon, she vowed.

Stuart came to see her every afternoon or evening without fail. He looked thinner and his face had aged by lines of worry but he soon began to look his normal self as the days passed in her company.

They were good companions, laughing and joking and even resorting back to their old familiar arguments, but never once with the vindictiveness or sarcasm or with the desire to hurt which had been present before.

At times, when Cindy would get tired, they would sit in companionable silence and, every now and then, she would look over at him only to find him looking at her in an odd unreadable way, an expression in his eyes that she had never seen before. With her heart beating much too fast, she would quickly turn her gaze away from him and concentrate on peeling an orange or apple or pour herself a glass of water which she didn't really want.

Sometimes at the week-ends, Stuart would get permission to take her for a drive out in the country further up North where the more tropical scenery left Cindy sitting in awed silence.

The time came eventually when Cindy could walk some considerable distance without any aid whatsoever.

As excited as a child who had been given something rare and precious, she showed off proudly, but awkwardly, to Stuart by walking slowly down the hospital corridor to meet him.

'Isn't it terrific?' she laughed.

'It's great, honey.' Stuart bent and brushed her cheek with his lips, the only personal gesture he had made to her since that first meeting in the hospital.

'Can we go outside?' she asked, her eyes glowing. 'Out onto the grass. I've got some wonderful news to tell you. The nurse will let me — go out on the grass, I mean.'

'Sure, why not?'

'Isn't it a glorious day?' Cindy breathed, shutting her eyes and lifting her face to the breeze and sun. She opened her eyes and smiled up at Stuart but immediately she felt a sharp twinge of pain at seeing his expression harden as he turned his face away from her. It was something he was doing quite a lot of, of late.

'Stuart, is something wrong?'

He smiled briefly. 'No. Why should there be?'

Cindy shrugged. They walked on in silence for a bit, across the green stretch of grass towards the trees to where a seat remained vacant beneath them.

'Please, may we sit down for a while?' She sat

down thankfully on the wooden bench. 'Stuart,' she looked down at her hands on her lap. 'You don't have to come, you know.'

'Come?'

'Come to see me — if you don't want to. I mean it must be pretty dull for you, coming here every day for the last month.'

'Look, if you don't want me to come you need only say the word!' Stuart snapped.

'No, it's not that. I just thought . . .'

'Do you want me to come or not?'

'Yes, of course . . .'

'Then that's settled, isn't it?'

Cindy remained silent, feeling bewildered at the change in him and completely miserable and out of her depth.

He was growing away from her again and she was unable to understand why it was happening and was powerless to do anything about it. 'How — how is Mrs. Reefton?'

'I thought you'd know,' Stuart replied, being deliberately uncommunicative. 'She came to see you the other day, didn't she?'

'Yes.'

Silence.

'How is your new secretary coming along?' she attempted desperately.

'Hopelessly.'

'Oh, I'm sorry.'

'What is this great news you were going to tell me?'

'Oh, it's Jo and Keith. They've got a baby boy. He was born yesterday.' Cindy brightened and turned to him eagerly. 'He's gorgeous, he really is . . .'

'How can a baby, one day old, possibly be gorgeous?' Stuart said dampeningly.

'Well, not gorgeous really, but so tiny. They're going to call him Michael. Jo's so proud and so is Keith. You should hear him boasting — already.'

Cindy's laughter died as Stuart got impatiently to his feet.

'What are you going to do when you're discharged from here?' he asked after a moment of strained silence. 'Have you thought about it?'

'Yes — yes, I have,' she nodded. 'I'm thinking of going to Australia — when I'm really well, that is.'

'And when you get back?'

'I don't know when I'll be back.'

'What do you mean?' Stuart asked sharply.

'I intend to work over there. I don't know for how long.'

'And probably end up marrying some Aussie business tycoon,' he said bitterly. Was he thinking of Delia?

'No, I'd never do that. I'd never live in any country other than New Zealand.'

'Love would alter that conviction.'

Cindy shook her head. 'Never.' 'And never would I love any other man,' she added to herself.

'Whereabouts do you intend staying in Australia?'

'Perth, I think. They reckon it's very pretty over there,' she replied casually. She had come to this decision only within the last few days. She realized that seeing Stuart every day and seeing him drawing further and further away from her, she would be better off away from him. 'The further away the better,' she told herself, as if the distance separating them would help. Emotionally, they were as far apart as any country in the world.

'I see,' was all he said.

CHAPTER TEN

CINDY stood in line with the other travellers, her Passenger's Departure Card duly completed and held, ready to be handed to either of the two officers standing at the head of the queue.

Why were they so slow? Why weren't they moving? She sighed, only thankful that she didn't have to bother about passports and inoculations when going to Australia. 'Just hop on the plane and go,' the Travel Agent had told her. 'Any day of the week.'

She glanced at her watch. Eight-thirty. Two hours since she had rung through to her parents at Apiti, and said good-bye to Jo and Keith at their home. She didn't want them to come and see her off. She hated farewells made in public at railway stations and at an air terminal it would be worse. It was more final somehow, to be leaving the country than it was just leaving a town or city.

And it was three weeks since she had last set eyes on Stuart.

She had left the hospital shortly after she had told him of her plans to go to Australia and during the weeks that followed he had made no attempt to see her or contact her in any way whatsoever. So that was that! But nevertheless, she couldn't just leave without saying good-bye. So she had rung him about three hours earlier, only to find that he wasn't home.

Elizabeth had sounded quite exasperated, and rather angry too. 'Don't worry,' she had said, 'I'll see to it that he gets the message.' Not 'her' message but 'the' message, and she had emphasized each word as if to convey a certain message to *her*.

'Oh, don't think about Stuart! I wish this queue

would get moving. If I stand here like this much longer, I'll scream!'

'So you're still running away? Don't you think it's about time you stopped?'

She stood quite still for a split second and then swung around. She saw him standing there in a way she had often seen before, and that tolerant look on his face was also very familiar. That 'Here we go again' expression that he always used with her, as though she was a child always blundering headlong into impossible and silly situations without first giving it a little thought.

Suddenly, she was tired, furiously angry — and overwhelmingly happy too — but she wasn't going to let him know that.

'How did you get this far? You're not supposed to be in past those first doors.'

'When I explained the situation, the Officer understood and let me through.'

'What situation?'

'That they were going to take off minus one passenger. I explained that she was getting married and that in about a week's time, perhaps there would be a booking for two.' He was smiling lazily, and for a second time that night Cindy felt as though she could have quite cheerfully screamed.

'I don't know what you're talking about!' she said coldly. 'You'd better go, the queue is beginning to move — at last!'

'Well, if that's the way you want it, we'll get married in Australia.' He stood beside her and moved with the queue.

Cindy gasped at him. 'What?'

'Do you want to get married in Australia?'

'No! I don't . . .'

'Good, neither do I.' He took her arm and began propelling her towards the exit.

They got only half-way when Cindy managed to

gather her scattered wits and stopped, pulling her arm from his grasp. 'Just what do you think you're doing!' By now the other travellers were turning to survey the scene with interest.

'We've got a wedding to arrange.'

'Whose wedding?'

'Ours.'

Cindy rocked on her feet. 'Ours?'

'Well, you are going to marry me, aren't you? The plane can still take off minus a passenger, but a wedding can't take place minus a bride.'

'B-but . . .'

'There's no time for buts.' He took her arm again.

'Now just a darn minute!' Again Cindy tried to pull her arm free, but this time he retained his hold. 'I wouldn't marry you if . . .' she began strongly and then broke off. 'My luggage is on that plane!' she wailed.

'No, it isn't.'

'What?'

'You heard. I had it taken off.'

'Well, of all the . . .!' But she didn't quite finish, for he pulled her into his arms and kissed her soundly in front of all the amused onlookers.

'Yes, darling. I know how you feel,' he smiled down at her bemused face, 'but save the endearments until we're out of here — and alone.'

'Ohhh!' She pulled out of his arms, her eyes glittering furiously. She threw the Passenger's Card, which she had unwittingly crushed in her hands, at his smiling face.

'I'm not going anywhere with you! And I'm certainly not going to marry you!' She didn't really care who heard her. 'You're ruthless, arrogant, moody, uncaring, bad-tempered and . . .'

'You love me . . .'

'I certainly do not!'

'As I love you . . .'

'I — I . . .'

'And we're going to get married.'

Cindy's face crumpled and her arms hung limply at her sides. Why was he doing this to her? She was so tired she wanted to cry. She felt his arm go around her, but this time she made no move to draw away. She stood limp, all the fight drained out of her.

'Why did you do it?' she asked wearily when they were seated in Stuart's car, parked in the airport's car park, deserted of people.

'Well, I had to prevent you from going somehow, and come with me.'

'And all that carrying-on just because you considered it time I stopped — "running away".'

'No! Because I considered it about time I stopped running away from the fact that I loved you. It's true that I'm moody, bad-tempered and so on, but I'm not uncaring. I care for you very much.'

'Is that why you haven't been near me during the past three weeks — because you cared so much?' she snapped, determined that after all he had put her through he wasn't going to get off so lightly. He had been so sure of her — all the time! Well, now she was going to make him sweat a little.

'I began caring right from the beginning, but I never wanted to admit it . . .'

'Until now?'

'Until now.'

'Now it suits you to admit it. How very convenient!' She looked at him coldly. 'Isn't it too bad that it suited me — and still suits me — to go to Australia?'

All at once he sounded humble and less confident, even the expression in his eyes which she could see from the silvery light shining into the car was uncertain. 'I'm sorry. I know I've given you a tough time.'

'I never considered it a tough time, so don't give it another thought.'

'Cindy!'

Her heart lurched at the hurt sound of his voice and all at once she hated herself for making him humble himself. Humility didn't, and never would, suit a man like Stuart. However, she didn't answer, but sat, stiff, and looking straight ahead of her.

'I love you, Cindy,' his voice low and pleading.

'I don't believe you.' Was she trying him too far? Did she want to see just how far he would humble himself? Or was she merely testing to see how strong her power was over him?

'Then perhaps this will help convince you!' he grated, no longer humble or pleading but downright angry. He hauled her none too gently into the circle of his arms, and she felt his lips seeking hers in a kiss which she had always longed him to give her, long and demanding, the anger drained from him. Beneath her hand, she felt the heavy thudding of his heart and she knew. She forced herself to remain unresponsive and waited for him to lift his head.

When he did, he demanded harshly: 'What do you want me to do, Cindy? What do I have to do? Get down on my knees and beg you to believe me and say that you love me?'

'Would you — if I asked you?'

His face was inscrutable as he looked down at her for some time. Then he smiled, that old familiar, self-confident smile. 'No, because I don't think I really have any need to. You're going to marry me, you understand that? I'm not asking, I'm telling you. Now I'm telling you to say those three very important words.'

Dumbly, she shook her head. He was looking at her in a way that had the power to create in her that mixture of fear and excitement — only this time she didn't have to ignore it or try and quell it.

'Then it looks as though we're going to spend the night in the car park of Magere Airport,' he told her softly, his mouth resting just below her ear and his

186

ingers slipping through her hair, causing the clips to
all out on to the back of the seat and her hair to
umble down. 'Then you'll have to marry me, whether
ou like it or not.'

She shivered. 'That's blackmail.'

'All you have to do is say three little words and
hen — maybe — I'll take you home.'

'That's still blackmail.'

He shrugged, drawing her closer. 'Call it what
ou like,' he said against her lips.

THE OMNIBUS
Has Arrived!

A GREAT NEW IDEA
From HARLEQUIN

OMNIBUS—The **3** in **1** HARLEQUIN
only $1.50 per volume

Here is a great new exciting idea from Harlequin.
THREE GREAT ROMANCES — complete and
unabridged — BY THE SAME AUTHOR — in one
deluxe paperback volume — for the unbelievably
low price of only $1.50 per volume.

We have chosen some of the finest works of four
world-famous authors . . .

VIOLET WINSPEAR

ISOBEL CHACE

JOYCE DINGWELL

SUSAN BARRIE

. . . and reprinted them in the 3 in 1 Omnibus.
Almost 600 pages of pure entertainment for just
$1.50 each. A TRULY "JUMBO" READ!

These four Harlequin Omnibus volumes are now
available. The following pages list the exciting
novels by each author.

Climb aboard the Harlequin Omnibus now! The
coupon below is provided for your convenience in
ordering.

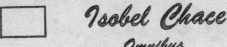

Isobel Chace

Omnibus

A writer of romance is a weaver of dreams. This is true of ISOBEL CHACE, and her many thousands of ardent readers can attest to this. All of her eagerly anticipated works are so carefully spun, blending the mystery and the beauty of love.

. . . . CONTAINING

A HANDFUL OF SILVER . . . set in the exciting city of Rio de Janeiro, with its endless beaches and tall skyscraper hotels, and where a battle of wits is being waged between Madeleine Delahaye, Pilar Fernandez the lovely but jealous fiancee of her childhood friend, and her handsome treacherous cousin — the strange Luis da Maestro . . . (#1306).

THE SAFFRON SKY . . . takes us to a tiny village skirting the exotic Bangkok, Siam, bathed constantly in glorious sunshine, where at night the sky changes to an enchanting saffron colour. The small nervous Myfanwy Jones realizes her most cherished dream, adventure and romance in a far off land. In Siam, two handsome men are determined to marry her — but, they both have the same mysterious reason . . . (#1250).

THE DAMASK ROSE . . . in Damascus, the original Garden of Eden, we are drenched in the heady atmosphere of exotic perfumes, when Vickie Tremaine flies from London to work for Perfumes of Damascus and meets Adam Templeton, fiance of the young rebellious Miriam, and alas as the weeks pass, Vickie only becomes more attracted to this your Englishman with the steel-like personality . . . (#1334).

$1.50 per volume

Joyce Dingwell
Omnibus

JOYCE DINGWELL'S lighthearted style of writing and her delightful characters are well loved by a great many readers all over the world. An author with the unusual combination of compassion and vitality which she generously shares with the reader, in all of her books.

. . . . CONTAINING

THE FEEL OF SILK . . . Faith Blake, a young Australian nurse becomes stranded in the Orient and is very kindly offered the position of nursing the young niece of the Marques Jacinto de Velira. But, as Faith and a young doctor become closer together, the Marques begins to take an unusual interest in Faith's private life . . . (#1342).

A TASTE FOR LOVE . . . here we join Gina Lake, at Bancroft Bequest, a remote children's home at Orange Hills, Australia, just as she is nearing the end of what has been a very long "engagement" to Tony Mallory, who seems in no hurry to marry. The new superintendent, Miles Fairland however, feels quite differently as Gina is about to discover . . . (#1229).

WILL YOU SURRENDER . . . at Galdang Academy for boys, "The College By The Sea", perched on the cliff edge of an Australian headland, young Gerry Prosset faces grave disappointment when her father is passed over and young Damien Manning becomes the new Headmaster. Here we learn of her bitter resentment toward this young man — and moreso. the woman who comes to visit him . . . (#1179).

$1.50 per volume

Susan Barrie

Omnibus

The charming, unmistakable works of SUSAN BARRIE, one of the top romance authors, have won her a reward of endless readers who take the greatest of pleasure from her inspiring stories, always told with the most enchanting locations.

. . . . CONTAINING

MARRY A STRANGER . . . Doctor Martin Guelder sought only a housekeeper and hostess for his home, Fountains Court, in the village of Herfordshire in the beautiful English countryside. Young Stacey Brent accepts his proposal, but soon finds herself falling deeply in love with him — and she cannot let him know . . . (#1043).

THE MARRIAGE WHEEL . . . at Farthing Hall, a delightful old home nestled in the quiet countryside of Gloucestershire, we meet Frederica Wells, chauffeur to Lady Allerdale. In need of more financial security, Frederica takes a second post, to work for Mr. Humphrey Lestrode, an exacting and shrewd businessman. Almost immediately — she regrets it . . . (#1311).

ROSE IN THE BUD . . . Venice, city of romantic palaces, glimmering lanterns and a thousand waterways. In the midst of all this beauty, Catherine Brown is in search of the truth about the mysterious disappearance of her step-sister. Her only clue is a portrait of the girl, which she finds in the studio of the irresistably attractive Edouard Moroc — could it be that he knows of her whereabouts? . . . (#1168).

$1.50 per volume